Ravencroft Springs

—EST. 1804—

PRO SE PRESS

RAVENCROFT SPRINGS
A Pro Se Press Publication

Edited by - Jessica Fleming, John Sterling, and Morgan Minor
Editor in Chief, Pro Se Productions - Tommy Hancock
Submissions Editor - Barry Reese
Director of Corporate Operations - Morgan Minor
Publisher & Pro Se Productions, LLC-Chief Executive Officer -
Fuller Bumpers

Cover Art by Adam Shaw
Print Production and Book Design by Percival Constantine
E-Book Design by Russ Anderson
New Pulp Logo Design by Sean E. Ali
New Pulp Seal Design by Cari Reese

Pro Se Productions, LLC
133 1/2 Broad Street
Batesville, AR, 72501
870-834-4022

proseproductions@earthlink.net
www.prose-press.com

RAVENCROFT SPRINGS

LOGAN L. MASTERSON

PRO SE PRESS

For Jennifer Fae Masterson and Sue S. Gabbard, for believing, even if they weren't certain of just what they believed in.

And For D. Alan Lewis, Nikki Nelson-Hicks, John Sargent, and Julianna Robinson for their aid in finding my story and my voice.

One

"Leave it, David," Marlow shouted over the din of eighties rock. He'd been my safety for years, but recent events had left me with a hair trigger. I was becoming too much for even my best friend.

I snarled in my aggressor's face. I was lean, and taught, and had him by the shirt collar. My right fist hovered over my shoulder, twitching to launch.

"Seriously, dude," Marlow went on. "This kid's nobody. Just let it go."

The guy's friends stood behind him, shifting and fidgeting in discomfort. I shoved him back into the bar and watched him scurry off with his posse.

After a deep breath, I slid a fifty and a predatory smile across the bar. The pretty, boring blonde on the other side returned the smile wanly.

Two hours and three bars later, we'd settled in at a biker joint on Nashville's outskirts. The music was better, the beer was cheaper, and the place was almost empty.

"Look," I told my buddy, "the town is tiny, all but dead. It's way up in the hills, away from everything. It's perfect."

"It's not perfect, David. Sounds like hell to me."

My brow furrowed, but I didn't lash out. "It's what I need. I have to get away from this town, away from that life. I can feel it, pulling at me like an undertow, but we both know I can't go back."

"Yeah, but—"

I waved my hand and went to the head. It was a lot like

1

the rest of the bar: matte black walls and dingy everything. I could almost see the black mold growing across the cracked mirror. My eyes were bloodshot, but the only adjective I found was 'dead.'

I stopped at the bar on my way back, setting two fresh beers on the gouged tabletop when I returned. "Look," I told him, "I don't expect you to understand me, or this decision, but it sure would be nice if you'd pretend."

"David, come on," he said. "Come on! Ravenscraw Falls? Is that even on a map? You need people."

"People don't need me," I replied too grimly, in no mood to correct him. "At least not now. Mary didn't need me. Looks like Sophie didn't either."

Marlow shot me a glare over the rim of his glass. "Mary might not, but your daughter definitely needs you, man. What's little Sophie supposed to do without a father? Don't you dare cop out on that one!"

But I did. I copped out. Two weeks later Marlow was helping me load the Corvair. Dropping the last box of books into the wagon's ass-end, he sighed before slamming the hatch.

"Why do you still drive this thirty-year-old piece of shit? Your novel sold three-hundred thousand copies!"

"Did it?" I asked absently, looking up at the gray door of my one-bedroom apartment.

"Whatever, David. Listen, good luck up there. Write something great."

He wasn't just my best friend, he was my agent. James Marlow had been a Music Row agent, and signed a lot of not quite successful artists before turning his back on musicians and moving on to literature. I had laughed when he told me; Marlow had never been a reader. But he had gone to college in New York, and he knew a lot of people. We talked about it for months before he quit his job at the label and set off to his old stomping grounds. I told him everything I knew about the current sellers, which hadn't been much, really, but it helped him figure out what he liked. Fourteen months later, I signed a contract making Marlow my agent. Three months after that, he sold his second book and my first, "Bleeding Edge."

He shook my hand, our eyes meeting only furtively, and he turned and walked off. It was quick: I had become unbearable.

I left the little apartment behind with the furniture still in it. I took some clothes, some books, my laptop, a few nick-knacks, and my swords. A liquor box held the kitchen stuff. The bathroom was in a milk crate. The rest had gone to friends and family. I didn't think I'd need comic books and video games in the mountains.

As the Corvair rattled onto the interstate, I slapped an O.M.D. disc in the player and lit a cigarette. It was a long road from the Nashville suburbs to Ravencroft Springs, but the travail was lightened by a document in my briefcase deeding me the owner of the Meadlynn Building, a fine limestone structure at the edge of the downtown district.

The term downtown borders on hyperbole. Ravencroft once held thirty thousand inhabitants before the great depression. It now stood all but empty.

I pulled in to the gravel patch beside my building, perched unsteadily over Black Ridge Road, a block and a story above Main Street. Three floors composed it, with two apartments above a retail space, all currently unoccupied. External stairs wound up to the second story from the parking lot, and I hauled my laptop and briefcase up. The key stuck in the knob. I sighed and trudged back down to the car, glad of the cool October air. Not finding any WD40, I went for olive oil and worked my way creakily back up. Eventually the key turned, the door screeched open. Stepping inside, I was impressed immediately by a musty odor and a brief vertigo. The shadows almost seemed to crawl about the space, not flitting, but oozing, warping, distending.

Leaning against the wall, I steadied myself and hit the light switch, an old two-button affair mounted on top of peeling wallpaper. Nothing happened. I had called ahead to all the utilities, but of course they weren't going to change light bulbs or clean toilets.

There was just enough light to reveal the round dining table, upon which I set my briefcase to withdraw a flashlight. Switching it on, I screamed.

The beam revealed a figure, standing by the wide front window, in the far corner of the open dining room/living room combo. It wore fatigues, but was covered almost entirely in moss, mold and some sort of pale, rubbery fungus. Two dusty gas mask lenses stared out from under a World War II infantry helmet.

I took a deep breath and coughed the thick air back out again. Then I laughed. It was short, and it didn't make me feel any better.

There was a bulb socket mounted above the table, so I went back down the stairs for the milk crate, where light bulbs nested with razors and toothpaste. The light flickered on and popped dead as I screwed it in. Punching the switch off enabled the second operation to succeed; the light revealed black mold on the ceiling and sent bugs slithering into recesses everywhere.

I explored the building. Steep, narrow internal stairs led up and down from a hall across from the door. The kitchen and bathroom were in the back. The icebox was barely electric, but worked. There were some condiment jars inside, including some Helmann's from the eighties, and mason jars filled with what looked like pickled gizzards. The bathroom was a nightmare of black mold and broken tile. The mirror was a mottled slate gray, anything but reflective. I caught myself staring at it in spite.

Upstairs was dryer, but drafty, with two large bedrooms and a storage room in the back, which had stairs leading up to the roof. From there, I surveyed the town in afternoon's fading light. It was beautiful in a sad way.

Driving through I had seen one by one what was now displayed whole-cloth. The town was almost abandoned. Housing enough to serve maybe fifteen hundred people stood vacant. In the town below and the mountainside about lived maybe two-hundred souls. The bank had been closed for years, and the nearest grocer was over an hour away in Banner Hill.

Main Street and the surrounding blocks were built up densely in spite of the rocky terrain. The business buildings and row houses leaned in on one another. The town was stone and brick—some of the streets still cobbled—and featured stretches of covered sidewalk and little plazas tucked in between a road system like scattered ribbons. Most of the shops bore fading signs, some dating back to the sixties. Across Main, the land rose up and a few small houses were visible among resurging forest.

The town itself was rich with trees, all just beginning to turn their leaves from summery green to that exquisite mélange of brilliance that only an East Tennessee autumn can offer. Brown forerunners dotted the streets, the sidewalks and roofs.

I watched as the flickering neon 'open' sign in the dingy window of Honeycutt's, the general store, flicked off with finality. The bent, ancient woman the realtor had called "Cordelia" hobbled to her old Ford. A belt screamed out when she started it up, but a stomp on the accelerator silenced it and the hag drove up Main Street, past the abandoned bank, past the crumbling town hall and the Spring House Hotel before vanishing over a ridge.

As far as I could tell, I was alone in Ravencroft.

Two

I met Cordelia the following misty morning. Her left eye was lazy, her shoulders almost impossibly bent, and her hands gnarled like vines grown through a wire fence. Her voice was deeper than I had expected, and gravelly. The shop's interior was dingy and smoke-stained.

"Mornin', young fella," she greeted me, cigarette smoke curling around her blue-gray hair. "Lookin' fer anythin' particular?"

I smiled wanly. "No ma'am, just looking around." I felt unaccountably like a teenager.

She huffed. "Suit yerself." A click punctuated her dismissal and was in turn followed by Haydn's Russian Quartets ascending from a tinny speaker.

I browsed the shelves of canned goods and paper plates, motor oil and phone cords, watching Cordelia bob her head in time to the music. There were hammers and pickled pig's feet. In the back, next to a Pepsi machine adorned with a yellowed 'out of order' sign, was a shelf of antiques, including old oil lanterns, square nails and jars of what could only be the organs of small animals.

I approached the counter with three cans of Vienna Sausages and a box of saltines. It was a pleasant shock to pay only three dollars, but I did, and left the store. Taking in the crisp October morning, I heard a string instrument join the speaker inside the store. Through the grimy window, I could barely make out the old woman playing a dilapidated cello. The chords she played seemed slightly out of tune, almost flat, but her gnarled hands moved with confidence. There was a quiet smile on her lined face. As the movement ascended, her bow swished and streaked until the final long draw that accompanied the crescendo. The open sign hanging just above her spot behind the counter flickered and went out. Cordelia rose from her stool and shuffled away into the back room, never seeming to notice me watching. I walked on.

Down a few doors from Honeycutt's, a pair of old men sagged a rotting wooden bench by a cracked barber pole, streaked not just with red and white, but with vertical drips of something greenish black. They eyed me unabashedly as I moseyed down Main, looking into the windows of empty storefronts. Some of them still bore signs, though faded and spotted with moss. "Forevermore Antiques," one read, and inside was a tremendous clutter of ancient wonders, all going slowly to rot. Something glimmered from the back, but I was unable to make it out through the thick, dirty panes of the window. The door was green, and had been painted more recently than its surroundings.

Next door had been a bookshop, and I cringed at the horror within: the books had swollen with moisture, and many shelves had given way, tumbling their contents into piles on the floor. Everything was brackish. The overhang was dripping green water, slow and painstaking, as though to build stalactites.

Another block down, a few cars sat in the gravel lot of what had once been a feed store but now served as the town watering hole. Across the street was the first real sign of life I'd seen since my arrival: a restaurant.

Ophelia's was a bustling old-school country cafe. Three men left the place as I approached, offering nods of greeting as they crossed to their old van. A sign on the door, written in red, green and orange glitter on black paper declared the restaurant 'Closed 10-21 through 1/1 - Happy Holidays.'

A long counter, washed-out blue with chrome edging, ran the length of the interior. Several men sat there, gulping down hot coffee and greasy southern breakfasts prepared by a big fellow with a pronounced limp.

"Hey, hon! Have a seat anywhere," invited the waitress as she buzzed by with a tray of coffee and juice. A supply truck pulled up outside. I watched her hustle around the little dining room, about half-filled with locals. She wore a white skirt and blouse with a red-checked apron and green pumps. Upon her right ring finger was a silver antique set with a red stone.

She seemed younger than me, maybe twenty-two. Green eyes flecked with amber sparkled under pale brows and her hair was white-blonde, cut shorter than I would normally find attractive. Her expressions were a little awkward, but not forced.

She was gorgeous. For a second I imagined her smiling only for me, but then there was Mary's scornful face, glaring up out of my memory. I read the waitress' nametag as she approached with order pad in hand: Cassandra.

She opened her mouth to speak when the bells on the front door jingled. We both looked as the deliveryman came in, pushing a dolly of boxes. She held up a finger to indicate that she would return shortly.

The boxes were soon shoved in the freezer or under the counter. She returned.

"Apologies," she said. Her voice was throaty but smooth. "We got the best coffee in town." It was the wink that got me.

The food was decent, much what I expected. I ate slowly, taking in the atmosphere. Two guys maybe just out of high school boisterously occupied the booth in the back. An old couple sat up front by the window, almost dozing over their coffee. The man was missing both ears. I stopped eating when I noticed. The physicality of it stole my appetite.

"Pie?"

"No thanks." I wanted to keep her there. "What time do you close?"

"Oh, about two. No one who lives here eats dinner out, you know." She winked again and said, "The bar opens at three." We laughed together, then I left her an eight dollar tip and walked down the main drag a few blocks farther, turned up Spring Street toward home, and stopped short.

In front of a neatly kept brown and cream Victorian cottage just behind the last big downtown building, stood an oval sign that read 'Providence House, Museum & Library.'

The door squeaked open and I entered a Southern parlor turned historical bazaar. The wide windows let in light enough to see floor-to-ceiling glass cases filled with artifacts and antiques, each named and detailed on a faded card.

'Flint Arrowheads - primary weapon of local Indian tribes - $1'

'Miner's Helmet - protected the head and provided light to a worker in the Wardlaw Copper Mines - works! -$20'

'Brass Miniature of Dunmore House - crafted by Edward Buchanan in 1972, this one of a kind sculpture captures the home of Davieson Morgan Dunmore, mayor of Ravencroft Springs from 1923 to 1929. - $170'

I examined these and other items of local significance for some time, but no-one came out. A rope hung across the stairs with a sign declaring the upstairs 'Private.' The sign above the hallway door read 'Library on Right.' The hall opened to a dining room farther down, and there was a bathroom on the left, but I obediently kept right.

A side window let a little light into a small room full of paperbacks from the seventies and before. Finding the switch, I lit up the faux Tiffany fixture and followed the 'Nonfiction' sign into the next room, which was no larger, but had a wide counter along the exterior wall under a pair of windows. Two worn stools sat before it. The other walls held all manner of reference books, from an Encyclopedia Britannica (1963) to science books from the 19th century.

Unlike everything around it, Providence House was clean and in good repair, inside and out. The books, though worn, harbored no dust. There wasn't a cobweb or mold spot in sight. Even the air felt cleaner.

A Dutch door stood half open opposite the one I had entered, and as I turned that way there was a low rumbling sound. Suddenly alert, I approached warily. I heaved a relieved sigh as I looked through the open top of the doorway to make out a giant Bernese Mountain Dog snoring between a pair of red wing back leather chairs, turned to face a fireplace in the back corner. I knocked on the door frame.

The occupants of the chairs, a man and a woman, shot upright as their companion issued one echoing bark. The heavyset, bald-pated and bespectacled man bent to retrieve a book that had fallen from his lap. I smiled at the woman, who brushed her skirts and approached.

"Sorry to startle you."

"That's no problem at all, no sir, Mr. Dunbarton." She smiled at my reaction. "Oh, yes, Mr. Dunbarton, we know all about these parts. I'm Cara Brennan, and this would be my husband Michael."

The man approached, stuffing something behind his waist. He straightened his tweed jacket before extending a hand.

"Pleased to meet you, Mr. Brennan."

"Likewise. How have you found Ravencroft?"

"I like it so far, thank you. It's quiet."

"Mostly," the gray-bunned woman chuckled. "I'm having some tea. Gentlemen?"

"Please, dear."

I demurred, but was soon convinced otherwise. The bottom half of the door swung open and Arthur, for so the elderly Bernese was named, came to inspect me. The room had two windows, a door to the kitchen, shelves, and a small desk tucked in around the focal fireplace and chairs. Every surface was piled with books, none of them new.

Michael cleared some National Geographics off the desk chair and rolled it up between the wingbacks.

"Have a seat," he offered, waving to his own chair and settling into the 1980 vintage roller. "What brings you to our little town in such dark times, Mr. Dunbarton?"

"I just wanted to get away from the big city and all the

people and the things I knew and depended on. What do you mean 'dark times?' " I redirected.

"Well, you saw all the signs coming in. Anyone could see how changing times have cut this place off from the real world."

"That's a grim way of looking at it, Mr. Brennan. You wouldn't rather say that the town is suffering a depression? I mean, I've done a little research and it looks like Ravencroft Springs has a kind of phoenix complex."

"I would not rather say that, no, but then," he smiled, "I'm old and tired and I've been here too long."

The teakettle sang.

"How long is that, if you don't mind me asking?"

"I was born in this very room in 1923. Been here since." His laugh was a shrill, nervous sound.

"You like books, don't you, Mr. Dunbarton?" Cara had returned with a rolling teacart, a mid-century revision of Victoriana spread with a variety of cookies and an old, chipped tea set.

"I do, yes. I'm a writer."

"That's part of your decision to come here, isn't it?" She handed me a cup and saucer. "Help yourself to cookies."

"Part of it, yes." I smiled, knowing the expression would seem washed-out. Selecting a cookie with a pecan in it, I asked, "Do you have any books here to recommend?"

"Of course," she replied, her eyes becoming cannily sharp. "I think perhaps you might like to know a bit more about the town, and some of it really is fascinating reading. A woman by the name of Blythe Sullivan wrote 'Secrets of Unaka Mountain.' I'll get it for you."

"Thank you very much," I called after her as she bustled into the nonfiction room. "And the cookies are great."

"Why, thank you, young man. My mother's recipe. Here's the book; I'm afraid it's more than a little careworn."

"I'll take good care of it," I assured her.

"Oh, we don't doubt it," she smiled back.

Ten minutes later I had extricated myself from Providence

House.

After a meandering route home, I cleaned the bathroom and the bed. I dried my hands and sat on the bare mattress. Mary suddenly appeared in my head, but I shook her off and went downstairs for a lunchtime scotch.

I opened my laptop, stared blankly at the desktop, and closed it again. There was no Internet in Ravencroft Springs, and I knew I wasn't going to write, so I sunk into the battered old couch and settled in with 'Secrets of Unaka Mountain.' By page six, I drifted off.

THREE

Over the next week, I cleaned the rest of my building. There were now ladders and shop-vacs and all sorts of tools and supplies in the shop downstairs. The wallpaper of my apartment was mold-free and the whole place smelled of bleach. Boxes from Wal-Mart and Lowe's and the Shop Shop were everywhere, and the back of the ground floor was filling up with boxes too, each labeled with the return address of an artist or sculptor I had met on my book tour.

I had also scouted out the town and surrounding settlements, the latter of which were all miles off. Those moments when the blacktop turned into gravel always excited me. It was a blatant contrast to hurried life in the city or along the interstates, where everyone and everything had a purpose. The hills around Ravencroft were dotted with farms and follies, alpine lodges and rambling roadside shops, and each had outlived its purpose. The follies and nestled gardens went unseen, most of the farms were overgrown, and the shops were caving in on themselves. The lodges housed only opportunistic wildlife.

With the diner closing soon, I had to make a move if I had any hope of connecting with Cassandra. Only a week remained before that gorgeous woman left to spend the winter with family in Savannah, Georgia. The diner had fed me every morning since I'd arrived in Ravencroft, and I had learned quite a bit about the town from idle chatter.

Jessica Prater was mayor, for example, and the younger folks liked her and backed her hopes of making Ravencroft a tourist destination again. The older citizens, including Al the limping cook, preferred the previous mayor, who focused on public works outside of downtown, like repairing the roads to still-occupied cottages and cabins on the ridges up above the town center.

The guys I had seen that first day in the diner, the younger ones, were Wilton and Kaleb, the only two recent graduates of the Limestone Cove high school who had decided to forgo college and stay in town.

The three men who had left as I came in were Chris Calloway, in the shades, and Joe and Jabez Pelphry, the local public works department.

Al, the cook, had worked for Cassandra's mother before she passed away some time ago. Cassandra herself had run the diner ever since, a manager from the age of ten. During her school years, she had hired locals to cover while she was in class.

I had thought about that a lot, imagining the kinds of tribulations a little girl must have gone through running a business and trying to live on her own. It was clear that the little community was both tight-knit and cliquish; surely they had helped her.

As I watched her that morning, serving coffee to a cadre of elderly men, her youth struck me. I wasn't old, but I felt it, and was pretty certain I looked older than I should have. Somehow, Cassandra had stayed vivacious and fresh through fifteen years of living on her own.

When she came by to warm up my coffee, I threw the dice.

"Been coming here for a week now, Cassandra, and I've seen the same faces almost every day. How many folks still live here?"

"Well, the official count is two-hundred and forty-seven, but I'd say closer to three hundred. You get to know everyone, whether you want to or not." She offered that wink again.

"Must be hard to date."

She laughed. "A bit, yeah. Of course, every once in a while a tall, dark stranger wanders in to town."

With a chuckle, I replied, "I'm only six feet tall."

She smiled and poured the coffee before answering a hail

from the old fellows. I watched her go with a lingering smile, touched at the corners with guilt.

I finished my coffee and got up to leave. Wilton and Kaleb came in, the latter complaining about a long shift at the Lime-stone Cove Blockbuster. Wilton, the bigger of the two by far, shouldered into me as I walked to the door.

We both stopped. His breath stank. His teeth were stained with tobacco. I glared at him for too long before Cassandra chimed in from the counter pass-through.

"Ya'll sit anywhere," she said with an angry undertone. The toughs swung into my recently evacuated booth.

Cassandra caught me lightly by the shoulder. "I'll be locking up here by three. Call me Cassie."

I smiled and left, trying not to saunter. Walking the two blocks down to Spring Street, I leaned against the wall of the bar and breathed.

Fishing in my coat pocket, I retrieved cigarettes and lighter and lit up. As I stood smoking, I glanced around, taking in the details. The bar was brick, painted and peeling through layers of blue, green and white. The windows were dingy. On the sill inside the closest sat a quart-sized mason jar. Curious, I knelt and wiped the glass's grime away with my shirtsleeve.

The jar contained what I can only describe as pickled worms. Thick, pale, meaty filaments filled the jar, pressing against the glass along with some greenish fluid, black peppercorns and garlic. I recoiled briefly, almost falling on my ass, but threw out my free hand to catch myself. I rose and headed home, flicking the remains of my cigarette into the drain as I went.

By the time I arrived, I had almost convinced myself the jar didn't contain worms. I was sure it was intestines.

At two I showered again, put on a gray sportcoat over my standard black turtleneck and took many more deep breaths. Mary manifested dozens of times, but I shoved her face, her hands, and her disdain back into my subconscious.

It was Sophie's appearance in my mind's eye that almost put me down for the day. I flopped onto my Wal-Mart replacement couch hard enough that the Claymore hanging on the wall above it popped free of its bracket and fell. The heavy blade punched a hole in the other cushion, the pommel caught me in the shoulder.

I stood up again, went to the kitchen. The freezer light flickered on and I took a long swig from the sole occupant: a Stoli bottle. I put the bottle back and closed the door before I changed my mind and went for another draught.

Half a cup of coffee and three cigarettes and a coughing fit later, I walked down the hill to meet Cassie. She had just locked the cafe door when I came around the corner.

"Hello there," she smiled. "I wasn't sure if you'd be here."

"I wasn't either, to be honest. But I thought, hey, why not? You don't seem like the type to take advantage of a guy."

"Oh, you're a clever one, aren't you, David? It's David Dunbarton, isn't it? Author of 'Bleeding Edge?' "

I admitted it. "Have you read it?"

"No, horror isn't really my thing."

"Good," I answered with a laugh. "It's not really my thing either, but it seems to pay the bills."

"I heard it was good, though."

"Oh, you don't have to mollify me. I feel pretty good about it."

She tucked a wool cap onto her close-cropped hair and grabbed my hand. Following along at arm's length, I went with her up to the top of Main Street where it ended at Crescent Road. We turned right, walked up past the Spring House and took a left on Rookridge, a new street to me.

"This is even steeper," I panted, "than Main. Where are you taking me?"

"Nowhere in particular, just walking."

"This is not walking, it's hiking." My breath wasn't ragged, just labored.

"Oh, if you want hiking, come on then!" She turned right

along a side street. I didn't catch the name, but it was pretty flat. By the second block it had turned into a gravel alleyway.

"This is hiking!" She had hopped onto a low wall at the end of the alley. With a wink, she took my hand to help me up. We continued onto a rickety old staircase that led only to the foundation of a ruined house. Saplings had grown up between the fallen masonry and timbers. Almost everything was covered in moss. Fallen leaves crunched underfoot as we continued through what might have been a back yard, up a rocky ledge, and on into the woods.

She looked around to see me panting with my hands on my knees some steps below. "Come on, David! Just a little further and we can take a break."

I grunted and pushed onward. A few hundred yards later we came to a spring well. The beauty of it stopped me in my tracks. It was a half-circle wall of limestone and granite built into a natural stone edifice about fifteen feet high. The spring itself was about six feet up this rock wall, weeping gently right out of the mountain, slowly dripping down into the clear pool. I sat on the wall, lit a cigarette and dipped my fingers in the icy water.

Cassie leaned silently against a birch trunk while I drank it all in before finally approaching.

"Mind if I have one of those?" She pointed to my smokes.

"Sure." I pushed them over, watched her pull one out, noticing the clear nail polish and that ring with the red stone. "Light?"

I pulled my lighter out of my pocket, reached out and flicked it. The breeze died at just the right moment. Our eyes met as she inhaled. There was a spark.

"What the hell are you doing in Ravencroft, Mr. Author?" Her tone was curious but serious too.

I shot her a quick smile and an honest answer. "Escaping, seeking, working, recharging and hoping, but so far, no writing."

"Trust a writer to be as specific as he is vague."

We laughed, and I thought about kissing her, but went on

talking. Too soon.

"It's the job. Making up stories and playing with language for a living makes one an odd conversationalist. What about you? Why do you stay?"

"Well, most kids can just go. For them, Ravencroft is all they know. They make it into college, or run away, or just follow that big city dream. For me, it was different. I had absolutely no hope of leaving, because Ravencroft is all I have. I make just enough money to pay my utilities and taxes. I could sell the house, the diner, or both but they're not worth anything. Nothing here is. I can afford to own a car, buy groceries, get by. So, I stay."

I caught a falling leaf, examined it. "Well it qualifies as the road less traveled, I think. Would you ever leave?"

"I think so, if the stars aligned."

We took a long ridge-top loop trail back down to Black Ridge Road after that. She held my hand most of the way. It was sweet and naïve and I ate it up. I had come here to escape worldliness as much as the world. She dropped me off at the Corvair's bumper. She knew I was thinking of kissing her, so she squeezed my hand and kissed me on the cheek.

"See you at breakfast."

I laughed, thinking of a pick-up line. "You bet!"

Still grinning, I watched her vanish onto Spring Street. The breeze had picked up, but it was nice out. On a whim, I started the car, punched in an old Concrete Blonde tape and sat on the hood. Johnette crooned and ached *Poisonous Garden* while I smoked and thought.

Cassie was something else. I certainly hadn't come to Ravencroft Springs in search of love, but maybe that's why I found it. There was definitely something there, and she fascinated me. I had always been the emotional type, ever in search of deeper meanings and connections, but I told myself not to start thinking 'we' and 'us' too soon. It wasn't just that Cassie and I really didn't know each other: I was still twisted up with the other life, the life I had left behind.

An hour later, I was still out there in a romantic fugue. An engine stopped down on Main and two doors slammed, but I thought nothing of it. I lit another cigarette, but it was getting colder and I had just flicked it when there was a distinct crunch on the gravel behind me.

As I stood and spun around, Kaleb Macintosh slammed an aluminum baseball bat into my shoulder. His big buddy Wilton stood on the street a few yards back.

I rolled with it, but it still hurt like hell. The blow connected against the back of my left arm and shoulder blade. The pain shot across my back and chest, down my arm. My fingers tingled numbly. I chuckled through clenched teeth.

Kaleb stepped back two paces, momentarily surprised that I wasn't unconscious or crying.

"I reckon you boys don't know 'bout the S.C.A. round these parts." Stepping forward, I reached in the open passenger window of the Corvair and grabbed my renfaire Gladius.

"Never bring a baseball bat to a sword fight," I growled, trying not to laugh. Wilton was stepping up with what looked like a tire iron, so I decided to take charge of the encounter before things got out of hand. Taking a long step, I shoulder-checked the scrawny Kaleb before he could swing his bat.

As he went down, I stepped on his shin, wrenching his knee. He cried out with a pitiful sound, reminiscent of a mewling four-year-old.

Big Wilton swung a backhand blow with the tire iron, which I parried hard. The impact knocked the iron out of his still-formidable ham hock, but he was backing up. Behind me, gravel shifted, and I turned to see Kaleb charging in. I stepped obliquely to make sure I didn't get trapped between them and swung a preemptive strike against him, slapping his elbow with the flat of my sword.

When he clanged to the asphalt, I couldn't hold back any longer. I laughed. They reddened, and in the fading light, stepped in to pick up their weapons. I closed my mouth, hardened my eyes, and stepped forward. It wasn't discretion, but they left nonetheless. They mumbled furiously as they limped back down Spring. I waited 'til they drove out, locked up the car and climbed the creaking steel stairs to my apartment.

Inside, I stopped by the freezer to slug down a couple shots of vodka before hitting the shower. The water heater worked pretty well, and as I steamed my bruise, I thought maybe I'd just had the best day I never got in high school.

Four

I spent the next day, a Monday, taking it easy. I was badly bruised, but worse than the pain was the doubt. I knew it should have gone another way. A wiser man would have defended himself without demeaning his enemies.

The martial arts masters I followed were old-school traditionalists, but born of the modern era. Their own teachers had been the last generation that was called upon to prove its prowess. Those guys had dealt with cocky young warriors arriving on their doorsteps to issue challenges with depressing regularity. They had to step out to meet the aggressor. It was the way of things. Their students, today's masters in today's world, took a different stance, knowing that the best way to win a battle was to avoid it.

I hadn't been in a dojo in years, but that did nothing to alter the facts: I knew better.

Those kids would be back. I never called the sheriff.

I did busy myself with simple activities like designing the paperwork for the shop. In the afternoon, the sign arrived, and I went up on the roof to oversee the mounting. The sign, which read 'Constellations: a Fine Art Gallery,' was up in no time and I went down to have a look from the street before signing a check. It looked great against the limestone with brushed steel lettering over a night blue background.

As the sun dipped over the hilly horizon, I went in for a beer. The mold had somehow returned to the inside of my Kenmore fridge, but I ignored it for the moment and grabbed the brew. On my way back out front, I hit the new switch by the counter. The air outside was heavy, in spite of the crisp temperature, and redolent of autumn forest. I lit a smoke and stepped out into the street before turning back to see the newly lit sign. The letters were backlit in blue and silver by the tiny LEDs scattered over the background. All but invisible by day, in the dark they created a gorgeous constellation effect, within which shone Orion, Cassiopeia, and Lovecraft's Elder Sign among others.

I nodded and went to sit on the opposite curb, cracked and worn. In spite of its decay, maybe even because of it, I was coming to love Ravencroft Springs. Maybe my half-mad, Cinderella Man dream could become a reality. It was a long shot, but Ravencroft wouldn't be the first lost little town resuscitated by celebrity.

Mary's voice echoed in my head, checking that arrogance. "You're not Stephen King, David," the ghost of her said. "You're an asshole who nailed one book and forgot your family."

I stubbed my butt out, dropped it in the drain and headed inside. I was sore, and worse, I knew she was right.

Feeling better on Tuesday, I went back to the cafe.

"You all right, hon?" Cassie asked in a casual tone.

"Sure. Sorry I missed breakfast yesterday. Trying to keep the gallery from getting ahead of me." I glanced around and saw the three fellows with the van. One of them wore a gray jacket with a Unicoi County Public Works patch. There was no sign of Wilton and Kaleb.

"I understand. Coffee?"

I assented and ordered a plate of biscuits and gravy with bacon. The folks who came and went as I ate were mostly elderly. The public works guys were in maybe their forties, one in dark glasses, another with a camouflage ear-flap hat. The third was younger, unshaven and red headed.

When I left the tip, there was a note tucked in between the bills. 'I'll be back at three. –DD'

And I was. It felt like she just scooped me up. I was smoking against the gaslight post across the street. The lights went out in the cafe, Cassie locked the door and we were off, hand in hand, up the other side of the ridge. The October sky was low and pale, but her quick pace kept me warm and breathless.

After circling back around to the Spring House, we took concrete stairs leading up beside it, which soon became a pebbled path. We crossed to a small parking lot with a chain blocking the entrance from which hung a 'Closed for Season' sign, and continued along a winding park trail. There was a distant crack of thunder, and a few steps later it started to rain.

"Shit," Cassie said flatly.

"You know, it always looks so good in romantic comedies."

She laughed, grabbed my hand again and dragged me back the way we had come. We broke right at the parking lot, hopping over the chain and almost running down the steep blacktop lane. The rain came down with a fury.

We went into a steep curve, and I lost my footing, coming down hard on my ass. Cassie turned at my "ooph," and laughed to see me sprawled in the street, staring back at her balefully. She helped me up.

"My house is the first one up ahead. Come on."

She led me more cautiously another few hundred yards along the tree-lined street. The gate we approached on the right was wrought-iron set into big blocky granite pillars. The Historic Register sign declared it Dunmore House.

As the gate swung smoothly open, I took the place in. A set of marble stairs became a short walk that led to the front porch. The house was a big Queen Anne, though densely over-grown, and had once been painted in tasteful browns and greens, but was now camouflaged with decay. Moss and fungus clung to the walls, under the eaves, and permeated the air.

The front door, peeling forest green with a triangular window of leaded glass, opened onto a wide hall with wooden stairs. The interior had the same mold problem I'd been fighting in my own building. Something white and rubbery lived in one corner, but Cassie directed me to the left, into the parlor, which was dry.

While she went for towels, I looked around at the woman's chamber, marveling in the thousand tiny secrets it told me.

Paintings stood on four easels and in two stacks against the hallway wall. They were landscapes and portraits mostly, in an easy, comfortable style, but a few were daring, and almost all of them featured some tiny oddity. The eyes of one portrait were too deep, the leaves on a vine somehow sharp in another. It was subtle, but granted each piece an air of surrealism.

Through an arched passage toward the back of the house lay the library, which contained many more paintings but also books. Most of these were art portfolios and popular novels from the sixties and seventies. A few were penguin classics, and I was pleased to note that a newish copy of Jude the Obscure had actually been read at least twice.

Cassie threw some towels at me and turned a valve to set the gas roaring in her capacious fireplace. She had changed into black jeans and a purple tank top. When she flopped down on the sofa and put her feet on the table, I had just finished toweling my head and stopped stock still, staring.

When she opened her eyes and caught me, we laughed. I stood silently with the towel hanging from my hand.

"Penny for your thoughts."

"I was just thinking that it's nice to laugh with someone again," I lied.

Her brow furrowed, just a little. "Well then sit here and talk with me until the rain stops. Do you want a drink?"

"Sure, scotch if you have it."

She said, "Nope, just some vodka, tea or cola."

"Vodka is lovely." As she went to the kitchen, I lit a smoke and asked myself what I was doing there. Where was Mary's scowl? Where was her harridan fury? How could Cassie drive her out so easily, without even knowing it?

"Here you are." I took the glass tumbler, downed half and smiled.

"So I was married," I began, "up until recently. I'm going to tell you all this because it feels right. Stop me if you want."

"No," she said softly. "Go on."

A dramatic deep breath, then, "I did the book—which as messed up as it sounds—I did for my daughter, Sophia. I mean, a horror story for your kid is a little off, so think of that as a bellwether. Anyway, I started it and stopped it and eventually, it had to be written. It got out of hand.

"The character got into me, and I knew that I had to get him out somehow. He was perfectly human, you know, but damaged so down deep, so early and so often, that he was inhuman, too. Somehow, I stumbled on the perfect monster. He had some of my grandfather in him, and some of me. Too much of both, maybe.

"So I worked feverishly, constantly. The second time around, I finished it in nine months, revised it in another three. That's not fast, but even so I was working on it all hours, out in the city thinking, watching, feeling out the next page, the next murder. I got mean, withdrawn. Mary, she got lost.

"She reached out to an old flame and I caught them a week before the book tour. Sophie was watching TV that afternoon when I came in all charged up. The galleys had been reviewed and the critics liked it, well most of them. The dissenting voices were loud and clear, but I had been steeling myself against that for months. I saw them coming, you could say, and their snipes didn't get through the good stuff. Excited to share the good news, I burst into the bedroom and there they were, right down the hall from my kid."

I looked up from my glass and she was watching me closely, her forehead creased sympathetically. She withdrew cigarettes and a lighter from a box on the parquetry coffee table. I stepped forward from the mantle, accepted the offered smoke.

"So I quietly closed the door behind me, pulled her off of him, and threw him out the third floor window."

I smiled back at her guffaw. "You're kidding!" she insisted.

"I am not, Cassie." My tone was serious again. "The bushes broke his fall. I threw his clothes down to him and told him I'd shoot him if I or my daughter ever saw him again. When I turned on Mary, she was standing there in her bathrobe with hate in her eyes. I packed a bag and left. We met a few times after that, but she never lost that look.

"Then the book tour started, and I hit the road. I had decided to drive. That was a mistake. Anyway, all that summer, fall and winter I toured the states from Miami to Seattle. Mary didn't even bring Sophie to the Nashville signing. I was drinking a lot, driving hungover every morning and I looked like shit, but there were these girls, and..." I slowed, "I hope this doesn't make you think less of me. I slept with three or four girls on the tour. It was wrong, I know, but I did it. A couple of them blogged about it.

"That was all Mary needed in court. The irony is, it created this weird buzz and for reasons unknown, it actually helped the book sales. I mean a lot of hurtful and mean and true things were said about me, some of them all three. It wasn't sexy, it wasn't misogyny, it was just stupid, but people liked it somehow.

"I've been trying to figure that out ever since." I sipped my vodka. "I didn't come here to talk about Mary, though."

"Wow. That sounds like quite a ride."

"Yeah, pretty much. Now, I have to write another one, open this gallery and hope I can break even next year."

"I'm sure everything will be fine, now come sit." She patted the sofa.

I had gotten it out, told the whole stupid, sordid tale. I sat.

"What about you, Cass?" Maybe if I put the focus back on her, Mary would stay gone.

"My story's easy. I was born in rural New York, but moved here when I was three, in seventy-seven. I don't remember New York, of course. My folks were hippies going out of style, so my full name is Cassandra Fae Grimshaw. Anyway they came here to make an inn out of this house, which my great-grandfather left to my mom. But dad decided he couldn't take it I guess. Mom said he didn't last six months here. She heard from her sister that he got locked up a few years later, burglary in the city I think. 'Nother drink?"

"Yes, please. Smoke?"

"Sure." The bottle tipped into my glass, I lit her cigarette and our eyes met again. She held my gaze a moment, feeding the nascent electricity we were building. "So mom stayed. Dad never divorced her, never hassled us, so we just stayed. In the eighties we gave up on the inn and mom bought Ophelia's when it was still Trudy's.

"I worked there, went to school, grew up. I've thought about college, but if I left, I'd lose everything. I can't sell it. I mean, who would buy for any amount I could actually do something with? And the fact is that when I go see mom's family, I always get homesick. And don't tell anyone they're in New York—I tell people they're in Savannah. Don't want to be labeled a damn Yankee."

"Mum's the word!" Stubbing out my smoke in the creamsicle orange glass ashtray, I glanced up to see her watching me like a hungry cat.

My pulse quickened, which is how I like to explain the fact that when the lightning struck and the power died, we both screamed. Then we both laughed. By the light of the fire I watched her reach under the sofa and produce a flashlight.

"Stay there a minute," she said, vanishing into the hall.

She tossed me a second flashlight when she returned. "Take this and follow me."

We went through the library and into a mudroom at the end of the hall. She pointed her beam at a green door beside the hall door.

"Go down there, turn right and find the fuse box while I get some candles in case it doesn't work."

I shined my light up at her face, arched my eyebrow.

"Okay. Fine. I don't like it down there at night." She darted into the hall.

So I went, smiling. The stairs were solid but the concrete floor at the bottom had begun to disintegrate. I shone my light to the right and followed the wall until I found the fuse box, where the main had indeed blown. There was a box of old-fashioned glass fuses, and I replaced the burned-out main.

As I headed back to the stairs, my light fell into an old kitchen, apparently disused, across the hall from the utility room. There were shelves hung over an ancient sink and washing machine, and the light glared back at me. Adjusting the angle of my beam, I stepped forward onto cracked pavement and could clearly see rows of dusty jars, several deep. They were dusty, but their contents were like those other jars I had seen, all around town. These stood row upon row, stacked two and three high on shelves, the ancient woodstove's cook top, the floor.

"You fixed it! Great!" Cassie called from the top of the stairs.

"I got a gold star in righty-tighty," I replied and flicked my flashlight off. For a second I thought about what was in the jars, but when I ascended the stairs to that strange, beautiful woman, the macabre curiosity of it left me. She took my hand and led me back into the parlor.

"Sit, I didn't finish."

"You did not." I poured drinks.

"Mom stayed, but she died in eighty-four. She'd gotten sick several times that year, and finally died of something like pneumonia. She wouldn't go to the doctor, of course, but they said it was lung cancer at the autopsy. I got everything, for what it's worth. I was ten. Al pretty much ran the diner, we had some hired help, and he made sure I was taken care of.

"My romantic history isn't so interesting. I don't really have one. I mean, I dated plenty in high-school, fooled around and all of that, but never really loved anyone, never felt like I lost anything." She blushed then, a pearly pink in her cheeks. "I'm not cold. I have a heart, I think."

I did it. I leaned in and kissed her, gently, slowly. Her response was longing, but after a brief moment she pushed me back. The rain grew heavier, pounding on the roof, the windows.

"Don't," she said.

I stood up, stepped back. My jacket hung over a stool by

the front window and I went for it.

"Wait. I don't mean go, I mean there's something else I want to say."

Loosening my defensive posture with conscious effort, I turned.

"Look, I just want to tell you—and I need you to hear— that I want this." I nodded and waited. "When I look at you it's like you're the only thing I've ever really seen. But maybe...." She stopped.

I walked back and sat on the sofa beside her.

"Maybe you should go. Maybe you should forget about this, about me. Hell, maybe you should leave Ravencroft."

"Why would I want to do that, Cass?"

"This town is death, David," she was pleading, almost desperate. She wrung her hands and leaned forward. "You don't understand, it's not going to get any better this time and I, well, I don't know if I can ever leave. It's like I belong here, but what if you don't?"

"Look, Cassie, I'll be honest with you here. I don't know the future, and I'm sure as hell not a hundred percent, but I can do my job from anywhere. More importantly, I came to this town on purpose, looking to get away from one thing and find something else. I may have found it."

We looked at each other for a long while. She was tense, searching, but I was oddly certain.

"I'm going to go, but I'll be around whenever you want me." I squeezed her hand and moved to stand, but she pulled me back.

There was another silence. This one hung heavy as she peered into my eyes, then closed hers tight. When she opened them again, she smiled.

"Let's edit that sentence, Mr. Writer."

I laughed. "How do you mean?"

"That first clause has got to go. Just give me the last part."

"I'll be around whenever you want me?"

"Yes. Like that." She leaned in close, twined fingers around the nape of my neck. Our foreheads met. "Can you say that again?"

"I'll be around whenever you want me." The throatiness of my reply was unintentional.

When we kissed again, the sparks swallowed me whole.

Five

I woke at nine-forty, found coffee in the pot and a note. 'Went to work—have to close the place up. Call me when you want me.' Home and work numbers were listed below a smooth signature.

Tucking the note in my pocket, I poured a cupful of coffee, which Cassie prepared the same way at home as she did at the diner: stronger than any fluid had a right to be.

The kitchen was done in an old-school country motif. A distressed table sat in a corner, under a window, painted green, but scratched and dented to show white and wood beneath. An orange vase of the same glass as her ashtray sat on it, with three plastic sunflowers. There were few cabinets, and the appliances all looked even older than my own at the Meadlynn building. A Limestone Cove newspaper, three weeks old, lay atop a lidded steel trashcan.

Stepping over a spot where green-black mold crept along the tiled floor's grout, I wandered through the open arch into a formal dining room. A door beside me accessed the mudroom, while another open arch communicated with the formal sitting room at the front of the house, opposite the parlor. The sofas were literally covered in mildew, green and brown and black colonies of rubbery or leafy or feathery life grew on every surface. Black mold streaked a massive mirror, the old-fashioned frame of which had begun to disintegrate under tendrils of fungus.

I covered my mouth and held my breath. How could she let it get like this, I wondered, but quickly realized that this was way more house than she needed. Annual maintenance alone would swallow every penny she made at the diner. Maybe I could help.

These thoughts had distracted me enough that I forgot to hold my breath. The inhalation was thicker than the coffee and redolent with rot and a strange, deep forest smell I couldn't place. An image of the basement kitchen, full of mysterious pickled somethings appeared in my mind's eye, and I decided I had to have another look.

Once downstairs, I found a chain hanging in the middle of the area, and pulled it to release the light of a flickering old bulb. I could see another bulb hanging over the sink, and I went to turn it on, too, for a better look at the jars. They were covered not in the dust I had imagined last night, but rather in a gray, felt-like mold. It was thin and light and dry, and when I brushed some off a jar lid, it erupted in a puff just as dust would have done, but with a dank and unwholesome odor.

I picked the jar up, and wiped a strip of the stuff more carefully from the glass. Within were chunks of some kind of meat, pale and striated and packed in a bath of pinkish fluid. The next contained something equally indiscernible, possibly some kind of organ meat. The third, I nearly dropped.

Eyeballs. Dozens of eyeballs, optic nerves cut at about half an inch, floated in a red fluid, with strips of onion and bits of garlic. For all I could tell, and I examined this jar a long, long time, they were human. There we numerous brown eyes, and some green and some blue. Some were bloodshot, and a few were smaller than the rest.

I looked at a few more jars, but stopped when my hands began to shake. They contained all manner of meats, not one that I could identify as a known animal product. Not one jar of pig's feet, nor pickled eggs, nor plain old pickles. I found no jams or jellies.

My stomach began to churn, and I left for warmer pastures, abandoning my coffee cup among the mason jars, forgetting the lights.

I went back up to the ground floor, and on up the stairs in the hall to Cassie's bedroom, where we had spent the night together. It was dry and clean, though not without clutter. Cassie had probably occupied this room since her parents brought her to Ravencroft: a pink plastic jewelry box sat next to a small black and white TV on the dresser. Posters of the Cure and Jem hung over a mirror, the frame of which sported photographs of girls in sideways pony tails and bright print t-shirts.

It seemed as though the adult who lived in this room wanted time to rewind, or ignored its passing altogether. But the air was sweet, and the memory of her touch rose, welcome, to mind.

I sat heavily on the bed, lit a smoke, and tried not to wonder what it all meant.

The weather was brisk, and runoff from the storm sang in pipes under the sidewalks as I passed the Spring House on my way home half an hour later. The UPS truck pulled up just as I approached, so I unlocked the shop door and the day was spent unpacking and assembling fixtures.

The gallery was coming together. The electrician still hadn't shown, and I still battled the ubiquitous musty odor in spite of three dehumidifiers, but everything else was more or less ready.

The mystery of the jars crept into and out of mind. What were they? All over town, that's what. In Cordelia's store, in Cassandra's basement, hell, even in my own fridge. I'd thrown those out, of course, along with the rest of the kitchen's contents. It was fortunate that Cassie's basement had been so dusty, or fungal rather. Whatever they were, I believed her: there was no sign she'd been in that basement in months.

I called Cass in the afternoon. We talked for forty-five minutes, avoiding headiness and heaviness alike. It was a good conversation. Happiness was evident in her voice. Afterwards, I pinned the note with her numbers to the wall beside the phone.

That night, the wind was high outside, and I stood at the wide living room window, my thoughts wandering all over town. Jars of what, pickled people? What possible purpose could they have? Who made them, and why were they everywhere? And what about the teenage toughs who seemed determined to prove something? I thought, maybe, it was more than that.

When my thoughts turned to Cassie following a brief detour to my sad, old life, I killed my vodka, stubbed out my smoke, at hit the sack on a good note.

My dreams were troubled anyway.

We met again the next morning when I went down for breakfast. Smiling secretly at each other, I left a note in her tip to meet me at the back door in two minutes. She stuck her head out at the appointed moment and I kissed her deeply.

"See you tomorrow," I said and made my way over to Providence House.

The scene within was identical to my first visit. The lights were off again, so I made my way through the library rooms and found Cara, Michael and Arthur just where I expected to find them.

The business end of a double-barreled shotgun stuck out over the back of Michael's chair. It was disconcerting, but not threatening.

Rather than disturb the napping curators, I sat at the Nonfiction counter and looked over a book about mining, which featured a chapter and plates about Ravencroft Springs' own mine. Though the sign in the black and white plate read 'Wardlaw Copper Mine,' the text indicated large loads of lead were produced as well. There was also a reference to a natural cave and the resulting turf battle with moonshiners that eventually flared into murder.

The book I was returning told similar yarns about feuds between proud highland families, government men versus mountain criminals and even a possible Indian raid early on. Frankly, I found a lot of it improbable. Blythe Sullivan's telling had been mostly embroidered genealogy, folk tales. What I really wanted was the living history, and I was prepared to work for it.

About twelve-thirty, there was a loud creak. I turned around on my stool to see Michael pushing the dutch door open.

"Oh, my. Hello there, David." He looked tired, unsteady on his legs.

"Hi. Hope I didn't wake you."

"Not at all. The ol' bladder did it. I'll be right back." He went on through the fiction room. I heard him moving upstairs, and then a flush. Arthur moseyed heavily up to me and leaned against my leg. I gave the beast the attention he came for and waited.

"I was wondering, Michael, if I could talk with you for a while," I offered once the old man had descended.

"Sure, David. What would you like to talk about? And would you like to discuss it over tea or coffee?"

I laughed quietly. "History over coffee, please."

"Follow me, son."

Michael led me into the kitchen, where appliances ranged from the eighteen-fifties to the nineteen-fifties. He indicated a seat at a little round table with a faded blue and white striped cloth and set up a stove top coffeemaker.

"What kind of history, David?"

"I was hoping you'd give me your version of Ravencroft's most important events."

He replied with a chuckle. "Yes indeed, coffee was a good call." A few minutes later he handed me a steaming cup and sat down with his own. Arthur had curled up in front of the fridge.

"I know I'm probably asking a lot, but I get the feeling

that the book your wife gave me doesn't cover very much."

"To say the least. My wife gave you that book hoping it would bore you. I know it sounds strange, but she thinks most new folks should just go on their way. Hell, I don't know."

He took a long draught of coffee, rubbed his forehead, and went on.

"Ravencroft Springs was originally settled in eighteen oh-four. It had been explored a few years before; the valley is good land, and anyone could see there were minerals in the mountain. Something like a dozen families built here. It was pretty remote, back then when remote really meant something.

"A cousin came to visit in the summer of eighteen oh-nine and found the place empty. There were signs of struggle in homes, but it had been awhile. Most folks said it was Indians."

"What do you mean 'most folks?'"

"Just that nobody can say, is all, David. No one can say.

"The valley was resettled in Eighteen-Twelve, I think that was the year. Yes, that's right, the same year as Mr. Madison's war began. The newspaper clippings I've seen say that between fifty and two hundred people moved into this valley. They were all gone when folk from Erwin City came with arranged spring deliveries. There were corpses this time, but only about twenty."

"Mind if I smoke?" I asked. Something about his tone was giving me the rabid energy that foretold a story.

"There's an ashtray on top of the fridge."

I grabbed it, lit up. "Indians?" I wondered skeptically.

"Again, no one can say. No one saw, but it always seemed wrong to me. Maybe the first time, I don't know, but not in twelve, I don't think.

"It wasn't until eighteen fifty that some fellas came down from Massachusetts with a claim on the property all around here, the downtown area, where the valley meets the mountain. They had a plan and investors and all the fine stuff. The main man was an Englishman, name of Vaughn Wardlaw. By eighteen fifty-three they had a camp, and by fifty-five downtown was taking shape as we know it today. A couple years after that there was the railway, and the station and the Spring House Hotel and the lot.

"Those were the good years, I hear. 'Rowdy but hale times,' one miner said. The civil war mostly passed Ravencroft by. There were never really any slaves, no tactical value, but there was a fair battle at the mouth of the valley just after the state withdrew.

"Naturally, over the course of the mine's operation, a lot of folk got hurt. Since they were mining lead in there in addition to copper and whatever else I don't know, lots of men got sick. More than once the stuff got into the water, and dozens of people died or went mad within hours of each other.

"I mention it because the graveyard-down in the valley on the south side is something maybe you want to see. It's sizable. The oldest stones are still pretty legible, and mark those twenty corpses they found back in eighteen thirteen.

"Anyway, the mine ran for years in spite of that. It finally started to run dry, and Ravencroft turned back into a ghost town before the turn of the century." He laughed, and then coughed. "I never thought about it, but here in a few months I won't be able to say that quite the same way."

"It's true." I nodded.

"Oh look at the time. I'll have to wake Cara soon for her medicines."

"I'll get out of your way."

"Wait," he caught my arm. "There's another thing you should know, just so you can think about it. Ever since papers were printed in this town, first the Springs Bulletin, then the Main Street Crier and finally Unaka News back in the seventies and eighties, there have been a couple of recurring themes in the news.

"I know a little about your interests, David, and I'm sure they'll pique you. Go down to the archives in the town hall basement. Dig around."

Michael pressed a brass key into my palm. "This will get you in the basement door on the north side, the blue one. Go at night, take a flashlight, and be sure you're not seen."

"Why are you telling me to do this, Michael? Sneaking around at night?"

"Because it's important, David. And there's a story in it. You take care."

I nodded and shook his offered hand. Closing his front door behind me, I wondered whether there was still lead in the water.

Still, I fidgeted all afternoon, all evening. I thought about calling Cass, decided I'd better play it cool, and instead watched half of Metropolis on my laptop and re-read three chapters of Sagan's Cosmos before I finally gave up and grabbed my big mag light from the bed-stand. Maybe a nice walk would calm me down.

Descending the exterior stairs, I heard a noise below me, and looked down just as someone grabbed my ankles and pulled hard. I tumbled down, twisting to the right and bringing my arm up to cover my face. The big one, Wilton, came around from the front of the building as I hit the gravel.

Scooping up my mag light, I tried to get up before Wilton was on me, but he kicked me in the shoulder. The bruise erupted in pain, and my shins and back were pretty banged up, but I pushed myself to my feet anyway. Wilton went for a gut shot, but I smacked his fist with my club-like flashlight.

I was stepping toward him to finish him off when Kaleb snaked his arms under mine and locked me in a full nelson. The high-school track star was too wiry to shake off.

Wilton stepped in then and punished me with six slow, hard body blows. I couldn't breathe: I could barely see. Kaleb released his hold. I went sprawling facedown in the gravel and the little bastard stomped on my kidney, wincing as the impact wrenched his knee. He squatted slowly down beside me, grimacing defiantly, and scooped up my mag light. He yanked my head up with his left hand.

His voice was high and shaky. "Stay away from Cassie,

you goddamn..." here he paused briefly in search of the right slur, "...stranger, and stay outta our way."

I just couldn't manage to keep my mouth shut. "Fuck you, punk."

I woke up a little after three in the morning, my vision doubled and the left side of my face caked in blood. The ground was already obfuscated under a thick layer of foggy white. It took me a while to get up to the apartment.

I washed my head over the sink, examined the wound in the mottled mirror. It didn't look as bad as I thought it would, so I climbed into the shower before hitting the sack with a towel wrapped around my still-oozing head. The last thing I noticed before passing out was a wide patch of purple-gray mold returning to the corner of the ceiling over my bed.

Six

Lady Fortuna must think highly of me: I woke up the next morning. My thoughts were pretty clear, the double vision had gone, and the bloody towel was reasonably easy to remove from my head.

I didn't do much but bleed slowly and read that day. The thought of getting out of town occurred to me more than once, but pain dulled my motivation. I also picked up the phone at least three times to call the authorities, but always wrestled the receiver back into the cradle, considering what the sheriff might actually be like. "Better the evil you know," I told myself.

Tuesday was better. I managed to work a little in the gallery, finally moved the mannequin from its station at the front window up to the storage room. The effort was exhausting, given my injuries, and I had to shower to rid myself of moldiness, but I managed it.

With so much accomplished by lunchtime, I thought about visiting Providence House but decided to try another tack by waiting until after dinner. That way, the couple might actually be awake when I arrived. Instead I oiled my swords and dozed on the couch.

I woke a few minutes after seven, and carefully made my way down the stairs, my gladius tucked into my belt under my trench coat and a spare flashlight in my pocket. A black ball cap covered the gauze taped to my hair.

There were lights on inside, not in the parlor, but in the library rooms and kitchen, and upstairs. As I entered, Cara Brennan hailed me from the kitchen.

"Just in time for fresh coffee, Mr. Dunbarton. Come on back here." Her voice was cheery, her wave animated. Entering the kitchen, I could see through the open study doorway that Michael was looking out the window into the back yard.

Cara's eyes followed mine. "Honey, Mr. Dunbarton has come to visit." Her husband nodded in my direction and went back to watching the night. "Don't mind him, David; he's always introspective in the evenings. Take your hat and coat off David, have a cup of coffee."

I knew she would ask. "Sure," I replied. The coat tree was in the front parlor, so I was able to tuck the short-bladed gladius through one of the trench's belt loops and arranged the coat so the weapon hung unseen. With a sigh, I hung the hat on the upper hook.

The inevitable "Oh my god, what happened to your head?" Michael left his watch-post to see.

"It's nothing, I just bumped my head on a rafter in the back room," I said quickly, hoping to dull the old couples' concerns.

"That's not nothing, boy," Cara informed me. "Sit down. Michael, the coffee's ready." He set a steaming cup on the table for me and poured his own. When Cara bustled out in search of medical supplies, he sat.

"Are you all right, David?" he asked quietly. I petted Arthur, who had ambled to see what the ruckus was.

"I'm fine, really." He started to ask something else, but stopped short.

I glanced over my shoulder to see Cara rushing down the hall. The motion unsettled me, and I fought back a wave of vertigo. She set a basket full of gauze and scissors and bottles on the table and went to the sink, where she drew a pot of warm water.

There was no stopping her, and after a brief protest, I relented and allowed her to carefully pull the existing bandage away. "God, David." She gasped at the wound just above my left ear. "Your temple is bruised too," she informed me, dabbing away at the caked mess with a damp cloth.

"Who did this to you?"

I looked up at her and glanced at her curious husband

before answering. "Wilton and Kaleb. Well, Kaleb actually, Wilton really just worked my ribcage." I laughed and winced. Their faces were largely writ with concern, but there was something else, perhaps relief.

"Those little punks," Michael said, rising from his chair and bumping the table hard enough to slosh coffee.

"Sit down, Michael. Don't get yourself all riled up, now. The doctor said–"

"Damn the doctor. Those shits have done enough. Not a soul around here would miss them, Cara. Not a soul." The last sentence was sharp and slow.

Scissors snipped near my ear.

"There's no need for you to get involved, Michael. If they try anything else, I'll be more prepared, and will certainly call the sheriff."

"There's no sheriff here in town, David," Michael explained, "and they've got no reason to give a damn over in the Cove. If those two get the jump on you—"

I cut him off. "Really, Michael. I can take care of myself. They won't get the drop on me again." I sipped my coffee while Cara shaved around the gash with a disposable razor. Michael watched me carefully.

He finally nodded, "All right then, I'll leave it to you, but not without telling you the rest of the Ravencroft story, as much as I can anyway."

"You will not!" Cara cried, throwing the razor into the water pot. "You will not let this boy get involved in all of this!"

She put her hands on my shoulder, looked into my face with bright, sharp eyes. "You listen to me young man, and listen well. This town is a dangerous place. Only dangerous people live here. I know you want to say 'that's not true,' but it is, David. It is true. Even us, Michael and me."

"Cara, honey, that's not really how it is—"

"Oh, yes it is, Michael, and you know it." Her finger shook furiously at him. "Now you just clam up until I'm finished, then if this boy—this boy, Michael—wants to hear about it, you damn well tell him."

Michael sipped his coffee.

"Now David, Michael and I don't believe we're bad people, but we are dangerous." She reached under her apron and set a small pistol on the table. I reached out to pick it up. "Careful now, it's loaded with one in the chamber and the safety's off."

I examined the .25 caliber Beretta briefly. Cara continued, "There's a reason. You may know a few people round here who seem pretty decent. You may think Cordelia Honeycutt's a nice old lady who likes cigarettes and classical music, but you can bet there's a shotgun and an ax behind that counter. I guess you think pretty highly of Miss Grimshaw, but she's dangerous too."

Stifling the emotional response to leap to Cassandra's defense, I listened on, caught up in Cara's passion.

"This town is poison, David. Lots of good people come here and most of them leave. They leave because they can see soon enough that Ravencroft is good for nothing, and they leave because they're the lucky ones. A few disappear, David. Quite a few. And when I say disappear, I mean that one day they're not in town anymore and they're not anywhere else either. Their families come looking, but there's no one here who will talk to them. They're sent to the police in Limestone Cove. They hand them over to the Unaka County Sheriff's office. A deputy shows them the house, with a suitcase and a car missing, and their loved ones too. You can believe me when I tell you that they don't drive out of town with a change of clothes, David.

"When I say the best thing you can do is get out of town, you listen good. You're a likeable young man, Mr. Dunbarton, and there can be good work and a family and everything you want and deserve ahead of you, but only if you leave Ravencroft Springs."

She pressed a final piece of medical tape against my skull. "There. You're all bandaged up. I put some Neosporin on it and I want you to take the tube with you when you leave.

Here's some gauze and tape. I'm going upstairs now, to leave you two to talk in peace."

I watched her walk halfway down the hallway and turn. I could barely hear her say, "I'm deadly serious about this, David. I like you. I hope you'll take my advice." There was a quiver in her voice at the last.

Michael smiled wanly when I turned back around. He rose and cleared the triage kit off the table. I accepted the coffee refill he offered, and when he sat back down, we locked eyes for a good while.

I finally broke the silence. "This isn't just some overfed good old boy's network is it?"

"No, David. It is something worse, bigger and older than that, and I can't tell you what it is." He rose and got me the ashtray. I obliged his effort by smoking.

"I can't tell you because I don't actually know. I do know that for my entire life I've been threatened but never harmed. I nearly got out and went to college, but my mother fell ill just weeks after I started, and with my father dead, I had to return. While I was away I met Cara, and we corresponded. It wasn't until she had finished school and moved down to marry me that we began to see some of what is happening here.

"She could see patterns in what seemed normal to me, and ever since she saw, it got worse for me. There are quite a lot of people in town who just want to keep these things quiet, David, but we can't. We must not keep them quiet."

He took a long draught from his steaming cup. "I'll just get back to the story.

"When the mine ran dry, the town dried up too, but the springs didn't. In the beginning of the twentieth century, Ravencroft was reinvigorated by the healing waters craze. I was born here in that same boom, my father a hotelier and I guess he fell in love with my mother while she was still in school, back when the town actually had one.

"That's not important. What is worth knowing is that when the Great Depression came, this town was pretty well empty. A lot of people came through here looking for work.

My father kept us fed by fixing whatever broke around town, but most families weren't so lucky. People vanished. I never saw anyone abducted. I never found out what happens to these people, but it was an open secret around these parts that folks just vanish in Ravencroft Springs.

"But I do know this, David. When the Depression started to turn around most places, it didn't here. It just kept on getting worse. After my dad died in thirty-five, mom kept us going with vegetables and eggs. Just about everyone else left. Davieson Dunmore, he was the mayor, declared Ravencroft dead at the end of October nineteen thirty-nine. He stood right there like a round giant on the town hall steps and told everyone who remained to come with him or go their own ways, but no one was welcome to stay.

"My mother was quiet the rest of that day. I eventually asked her when we would leave, and David, I remember her exact words. I was sitting where you are now, and she was right here, and my mother said to me 'We're not leaving son, because this place is old and terrible but we are young and good.'

"We didn't leave. When Davieson came to see us, there was a serious October storm blowing, and mother met him on the porch with her shotgun. Even though they screamed at each other I couldn't make out a thing until the very end. It must have been the eye of the storm or something because the thunder and rain came back just a minute after the mayor climbed back in to his big black car, but it was long enough for me to hear that last thing he said."

Michael leaned in close and almost whispered to me. "That big bloated bastard said, 'You sure know your stuff, Angeline Brennan. I don't know how you know it, but all right. You just stay then, and good luck to you, but if I ever hear you tell anyone a thing, we'll drag you down below. And that's a promise.'"

"Well I didn't know what that meant, and I still don't, but the next morning was bright and pretty warm, so I went out to play. The town was empty. Doors stood open, lights left on. A house high up the ridge was burning, and there was no one to put it out. I wandered around the town on my bicycle, searched and searched, but there was no one.

"A lot of cars were missing, so I figured most folks must have gone, but when I rode up to the old mine entrance, I saw all those cars in the gravel lot. Over the mine entrance was a brand new wrought-iron gate. When I went to examine it, there were noises coming from the mine. I thought I heard screams.

"I ran back to my bike, but screamed myself when I saw what I thought was a ghost at first. But it wasn't a ghost, it was Cordelia Honeycutt, dressed all in white and painted white too. She grabbed me. I remember her fingernails digging into my shoulders.

" 'They left me here,' she told me. It was a whisper and her breath smelled like death. 'They left me here to watch you and your mother. And I will, boy. I will watch you both,' she said."

Michael drained his coffee cup and rose to refill it. In the silence I wondered about this man, about the place and the story.

"So what did it mean, Michael? Did they all go into the mine?"

"I guess they did." He sat down. "Listen, I'm not supposed to, but may I have a smoke, David? My nerves are standing on end."

"If the doctors said 'no,' then it's my sworn duty to say 'yes,' " I quipped offering him the pack. He took one, lit it, inhaled slowly, almost reverently. "Just don't let your wife catch you or we'll both have hell to pay."

He laughed and coughed once. "That's a fact. I don't know what happened down there in that mine, but this town is haunted, cursed, or something. I feel like my mother somehow set me up to be a last line of defense or I don't know what, but Cara and I aren't like them, David.

"Anyway, Ravencroft rebuilt itself slowly. I guess people just sort of moved in one family at a time. I was sixteen when the whole town vanished that Halloween night. I had to transfer to the high school in Limestone Cove, and I didn't really know any of the families who moved in before I went off to college, but there were only a few.

"Before I moved away, mother helped me earn the money I needed for school by selling off all the furniture and fixtures from the hotels and some of the houses. Only one of the hotels is standing any more of course, and even it's on its last legs. In town, of course; there are a couple up in the hills. Anyway, I drove off to Knoxville and started school, met Cara, and was just thrilled about a real life away from here when I had to turn around and come back.

"That was nineteen forty-one, and the place was still pretty much a ghost town. Farm families had filled in the valley and a mechanic opened up, but the town itself rotted away. It picked up again around here in the fifties and sixties, but by the late seventies the place dwindled again until it turned back into this.

"And so our little town is in Limbo or Purgatory or whatever you want to call it. We get a few visitors in the summer and a lot of folk from the hills hereabouts come for the Harvest Social, the only one left around here that seems to amount to anything, but Cara and I stay home."

I stubbed out my cigarette and Michael did the same, though reluctantly.

"You still have that key? Good. Have a look David, and decide for yourself. I have to take some coffee up to Cara. She won't come back down, and I suppose I'd better go make amends."

"Tell her I'm sorry if I upset her and thank her for the patch-up." I put on my coat, tucking my sword away, in the front room while Michael prepared a tray.

As I was opening the front door to leave, he called to me from the bottom step. "David, you know son, Cara's always been known for good advice."

"Thanks, Michael. I'll see you." I stepped out onto the street and looked around carefully before turning right and going down to Main.

That old couple had my head spinning. Was there something terrible going on in Ravencroft? Even if that mayor had been a charismatic madman, how did that account for the rumors and mysteries dated before and after his time? Was it lead poisoning or something less obvious? And why didn't Michael offer any details about the moss and fungus and mold everywhere? Only then did I realize it, but the home he shared with Cara and Arthur was entirely mold-free.

I walked up the hill toward the town hall. Michael wasn't telling me everything, and I was hell-bound to put the pieces together myself. I was about to unlock the blue door when I heard a rough-running engine approach. There was a rusting dumpster in the alley, and I ran for it just as the white utility van pulled off Main Street.

My breathing quickened and I struggled to stay quiet. The entire public works division, all three of them, piled out of the van. They went wordlessly around the back and opened the cargo doors.

The thing they unloaded and carried in the town hall's front door was a body bag.

Seven

By noon the next day, I checked into the Hotel St. Oliver in Knoxville with a well-packed overnight bag, my laptop and a trunk full of the things I couldn't bear to leave behind. In my room, I paced in front of cable TV for a while before sitting on the obscenely floral bedspread and scooping up the phone. Settling the receiver against my ear, I dialed the one number I knew by memory.

"Dorset Agency, Marlow Atchison."

"Hey, Marlow," I said, fishing smokes and lighter from my pocket.

"David, good to hear from you," he replied cheerily. "Hang on just a sec." From the background noise, I knew he was on his cell, at a restaurant, probably meeting a client.

I heard something like a door closing and the din subsided.

"Okay," he said. "What's up?"

"Oh, not much," I chuckled.

"How's Ravenscraw treating you?"

"Ravencroft," I corrected. "It's certainly been interesting."

"Really?"

"Oh, yeah," I told him.

"What kind of interesting? Book tour interesting?"

"Almost, dude, almost. I'll just say that the locals are plenty colorful."

"Well, good colorful or the other kind?" he prompted.

"Both, I think. I have a lot of work left to do, and I don't know if I can manage it."

"What, now you want to come back? Come on, David."

"It's not quite that simple, but I think maybe yes. I just keep having all these little problems, so many. There's mold everywhere, and, well, the townies don't seem to care much for me. And I don't mean your typical insular hillbilly stuff here, Marlow, I mean serious business."

"I don't know what serious business means," he said flatly.

"I don't either, dude. I know it means bodies carried around at night, and a documented history of abductions, and the occasional attempted ass-kicking, but I don't have the slightest hint of a clue why." I sighed. "Part of me really wants to figure it out, though. The rest, the bigger part, seems to think I should bail."

"Which part wrote Bleeding Edge?"

I sighed again. "I guess the part that wants to stay."

"Okay, then listen good. I think you should ignore that part completely. I know, you're shocked, but as good as that whole experience was for both our bank accounts, maybe you should avoid having another one like it." He paused, but cut back in just as I started to speak. "I know it's hard to hear, brother, but what you need is some god damn normalcy. That place is too small and too creepy. Maybe you should go stay with your cousin in Dallas or something."

"Nah," I said, "Rikki's got enough on her hands with the kids and Tom's leg." I stubbed my smoke out in the aluminum foil ashtray.

"That, David, would be 'normalcy.' You could probably help her out."

"I'll think about it. What's up with you?"

"Just the usual, you know, trying to find the next Stephen King. You seen him?"

"Nope," I said. "Not one word."

"Well, then I'd better get back to the soccer mom with the vampire romance."

"Ew," I exhaled dramatically.

"Call me again soon, David," he said with a chuckle.

I laid the receiver back on the cradle and stretched. I hopped in the shower, and when I opened my bag for clean clothes, the musty miasma of Ravencroft Springs poured out.

I put my worn clothes back on, and stuffed the rest into the hotel's laundry bag, calling down to the desk to have it picked up.

Then I went out. I had a quick Mexican lunch and went shopping. After picking up ten pounds of graphic novels at Organized Play, I yielded to the siren call of a billboard I'd been seeing all day: 'Kerbela Gun Show, October 22-24 & 29-31.'

I swung by the venue even though it was Tuesday. Having researched gun show society for a comic book, I knew the odds were good that someone would be there. Sure enough, I met a dealer and a security guard smoking at the entrance of the Shriner's Hall. Joining them under the concrete overhang, I struck up conversation and a couple of butts later we all went inside together.

"What're ya lookin' for, David?" Phil asked once we arrived at his booth, full of locked storage boxes. He was a short guy, with graying muttonchops and a blue tactical vest.

"I'd like a little protection, a lot of intimidation, and a dash of sensibility."

"I'm gonna assume that means you don't want a Kalashnikov."

"That's an AK-47, right?" He nodded. "No, I'm going to stop short of the assault rifle mark."

"Roger that, son. Let's start with the basics. Ya done much shootin'?"

"Not since I was a kid," I answered.

"That's all right. Lemme show ya some shotguns!" I smiled at his exuberance and we dug into the dealing.

It took about three hours to finesse Phil into selling me the goods I needed at the price I wanted. The Benelli 12 gauge was in my eye from the moment I saw it, but I did let him talk me out of a cheap .22 and into a Smith & Wesson 1911. A big box of ammo, storage cases, a holster, three spare clips for the pistol, and a cleaning kit rounded out my purchase.

As I packed my weapons into the back of the Corvair, we all shared one last smoke.

Phil asked, "So what does a fella like you want with that kind of ordnance? I normally don't ask, but you ain't my usual customer."

"I guess not. You could say personal defense."

"All right then, David," the scruffy veteran replied, "I sure hope it works for you."

"Me too, Phil. Thanks again."

Back in my hotel room, I visited the internet. Nothing had really changed in the wide world while I had been away. Not really. My email inbox was a nightmare, and I started to work my way through it while my subconscious laboriously processed that which I mindfully ignored.

After clearing out the crap, there remained only messages from Marlow, my family and my ex-wife. Rather than face them, I started writing. Fifteen minutes later, I shut down the laptop and read some comics.

It was impossible to concentrate. I kept wondering about all the things I'd seen in Ravencroft. Images of canned who-knows-what imposed themselves over the panels as I tried to read. I finally gave up and clicked off the light. With closed eyes, the inescapable questions raged like a thunderstorm. Who was in that body bag, and why the hell were public workers carrying it into town hall? Why was I unable to defeat the mold in my building? There were fungus and moss all over the town, and I knew the stuff had pervaded Cordelia's shop and Cassie's house, but the diner was clean. How could that be?

In the dark, in a strange room, a strange bed, I told myself I was just being paranoid, right before calling myself a liar. I sat up, lit up, and thought about my cousin in Dallas. Rikki was a good kid, a lithe dance instructor and confirmed nerd three or four years younger than I. Her life was pretty normal, with husband and kids. Her father, my uncle, had been a great guy, but he died almost a year ago. Ever since, her mom had stayed with them, avoiding the house where her husband suffered the fatal stroke. Then, just back in the spring, her husband, Tom, had broken his leg in a bike wreck, and broken it badly. Last time we spoke, she told me he was just beginning to recover at all.

As much as I loved Rikki, her whole life sounded like a nightmare, and I didn't think my presence was likely to help.

Moreso, I was developing three very important reasons to stay. I had my shop, which was a major investment. It wasn't a do or die scenario, but if it failed, I'd probably be getting hungry sooner rather than later.

I also had Cassie, that beautiful woman who had accepted me so warmly, who offered so much hope and mystery. But then, I could not hope to know what that would bring in the long term. Hell, I didn't even know what she wanted. Maybe, tactically, that was not a good reason, but it was pretty compelling nevertheless.

And bound up within that was the final reason to return to Ravencroft Springs. The mystery of it would not let me go, pervading every thought. Whatever was going on in that old, broken town, I had to know.

I couldn't guess Cassandra's role. I couldn't know if the jars in her basement were hers, or the remnants of someone else's life. Had she ever laid a hand on one? I had to find out. I had to know why she'd called Ravencroft Springs 'death.'

A pack of cigarettes later, I finally fell asleep.

Eight

I woke only a few hours later, pre-dawn, shocked awake by the horror of my dream. Filling my mind was that final image of it: my little girl, Sophie, was coming for me, bearing above her head the bloodied knife with which she had just murdered her mother. The military surplus mannequin I had found in the Meadlynn Building watched from the corner of our Nashville home.

I did not scream, but I did take a few deep breaths, switch on the light and get ready to leave.

I was on the road by dawn. My stomach recommended skipping breakfast, so I sipped at a hot mug of gas station coffee as I pulled out and made for Ravencroft Springs.

Once I reached the Unicoi County line, I went off the beaten path, or rather back on it, and explored the foothills of Unaka Mountain, the area surrounding Ravencroft.

Limestone Cove, the nearest town, wasn't Wal-Mart big, but it did feature two drug stores, a Blockbuster, and a hole-in-the-wall comic and games shop. I counted seven churches. There wasn't one in Ravencroft, and as far as I knew, there never had been.

I circled back onto the state road, and headed back west before turning off on the side roads one by one, checking out the countryside. Dotted with houses and fields, the side of Unaka Mountain was largely forested. Some of it had been harvested for lumber, but there was no clear cutting that I could find. In hours, I encountered only three other drivers on the back roads, one of whom seemed to be following me in an old black pickup. After a ten minute eternity, he turned off on a farm drive, and my breathing and pulse slowly returned to normal. I didn't know if the hill folk were anything like the townies, and there was no rush to find out.

The mountain itself was not high, even for the Smokies, but it was rich, and old. If it did not leap toward the sky like Everest, it had roots deep enough to touch Pangaea. The unfathomable age of Unaka and its many brothers in the Appalachian Mountains had always impressed me more than snow-capped peaks.

There were a couple of scenic routes in the area, one of which offered a view of Ravencroft Springs. It was distant, but gave me a better notion of the geography. Three- to six-story limestone and granite buildings snaked along curving roads, packed together close as vertebrae. The town's Victorian houses were set back, up steep inclines or behind moss-covered retaining walls, many all but swallowed by vines and undergrowth. I could also make out numerous crumbling structures scattered throughout the woods; abandoned homes and farmhouses. Only foundations and chimneys remained. Most were even without a path to the door or a road to the path. On one high knoll, the best part of a barn survived, its hayloft door staring like a blind, cyclopean eye.

The skeletal remains of a handful of hotels dotted the roads up Unaka's shoulders. They had been fine places, once in high demand. Now they lay like the corpses of great myths; one with broken timbers in the Bavarian style, now reminiscent of a ribcage; another, a great limestone edifice with collapsed roof and broken windows, seemed a fresher corpse. Higher up, the balds were pale brown splotches amid the woods. A peculiar feature of that ancient region, they would erupt in color come springtime.

I was able to make out the cemetery, too. No stony footprint betrayed a church's ghost, but a low wall encircled the graves. It seemed to cover many acres. There were a few obelisks and rising angels, but most of the graves were marked by modest stones, mere dots of gray from my position. The dozens of trees within the wall had already shed their leaves, and a handful of cenotaphs and three classical vaults stood out among them. Tucked away in a tree-lined hollow at the very back was a river stone cottage with a rusty roof.

Low, thin clouds skidded across the gray sky as I looked out, a lifeless contrast to the bright colors of the earth. I turned to look up the mountain, toward the bald peak, and a vast, deep shadow crossed over the red and gold woods. Looking skyward once more, I saw nothing there to cause it. I would have heard a low-flying plane, and there wasn't enough light filtering through the cloud cover to cast something so black over the landscape.

The temperature had dropped, as well, and I shivered, turning to the car as the wind picked up, nearly masking the rough-running engine of an approaching vehicle. My walk became a hustle, and I slid into my seat, cranked the ignition and threw her into gear in a real hurry.

As the gravel flew and the lookout vanished around the curve behind me, I told myself, one more time, that it was all in my head.

Even so, I resolved to follow Michael's advice, and wound my way back down the mountain and into Ravencroft. Turning left off of Main, I followed the winding Coffin Road about a half a mile before the stone wall appeared on my right. A rusting wrought iron sign spanned the entrance, naming the place "Scotsman Creek Cemetery" in ornate lettering.

I parked the car on the grassy verge, opting to walk around a while, to get intimate with the boneyard's denizens. Most of the graves were marked with small, simple granite or marble slabs, dotted with pale lichen. Some larger monuments bore names I recognized: Dunmore, Honeycutt, and Grimshaw.

As I wound my way along the crunching gravel tracks, enjoying the crisp air and carpet of colored leaves, I heard a low, distant sound. It was difficult to make out, but seemed to originate farther in, if the sharp ridges and sloping valleys did not confound my ears.

Making my way toward the noise, I passed through what must have been the oldest part of the yard, ancient stones worn all but smooth by long decades of exposure and blooming with dark purple and gray lichen. The soil was wet underfoot, loamy and redolent. Marking the location, I went on, past a cenotaph bearing the name Meadlynn, and bearing down on what I thought might be the cottage.

The whole place was dotted with trees and decorative hedges. Flowerbeds stood empty, not overgrown, and I slowed my pace, realizing that unlike most of Ravencroft, someone had an interest in taking care of this place. Not knowing who that might be, I became suddenly hyper-aware.

Slipping my hand into my trench coat pocket to thumb the safety off my pistol, I listened carefully to the noise, straining to pick it up. A series of low, long "ssshhh" noises were each punctuated with a thump. As I stepped forward again, there was a scrape. A few breaths later a sharp ringing sound, like metal on stone.

Unable to see anything over the steep hill I ascended, I cut to my right, and approached a long holly hedge, which I hoped might provide cover. It did, and a view to boot, because I could just see over it on the pads of my feet. I followed along a few dozen yards, and peered over.

Some way distant on a hillock, by an old oak tree not far from the cottage, a young girl dug a grave. I could not see much from my vantage, but she had long, dirty blonde hair and wore a faded flowery sundress. Her feet were bare, and as I watched, she squatted down to remove a chunk of stone from the hole. As the "ssshhh, thump" of her digging resumed, I located a gap in the holly and went through, taking my hand from the coat pocket to push aside an errant branch.

"Hello," I called from a few yards away.

She dropped her shovel and turned, startled. My reaction must have been obvious, though I tried to restrain it. She stood quite under five feet tall, and her face was a bizarre mix of features: honey-toned almond eyes and a fine nose sat between wide, thick brow and cheekbones. Her skin was pale and blotched with spots of subtle pink and gray. Her movements were sharp, as if she were uncomfortable in her thin but heavy-jointed frame.

The uncomfortable smile she offered revealed crooked, gapped teeth but also a hint of sweetness.

"Hello," she said slowly and quietly. "Who are you?"

I took a few steps forward. Her face was lined and her shoulders strong under the sundress straps. I knew she was older than I had thought, but her voice was somehow child-like.

"I'm David. I'm new in town."

She frowned. While I could not have described her as pretty before, the scowl aged her by decades and brought something feral to her demeanor. Fortunately, the expression passed quickly.

"Oh," she said simply. After a long pause, "Well, why wouldya . . . wanna go an' do . . . that?"

She spoke slowly, with awkward pauses and drawn vowels.

"Well, I needed a change of pace, I reckon," I answered in a vernacular closer to her own.

"Oh," she said again. Her left foot scooped at loose dirt the way a school girl might scuff her tennis shoe, eyes on the ground. Then she suddenly jerked upright, long, tangled hair dancing around her as she offered a grubby hand. "I'm Eleanor. Eleanor . . . Hopewell. Pleased ta . . . make your . . . acquaintance."

With her honest but uncommon smile and sweet southern drawl, she was kind of pretty, after all. I shook her hand and smiled.

"Tell me, Eleanor, why's a little thing like you doing a job like this?"

"Oh," she repeated. After another long beat, "Well, Ah may be . . . little, but . . . Ah'm plenty strong . . . and Ah care about this place, and who all's . . . here, and . . . what all goes

. . . on."

"I wonder if I could help," I offered. She accepted, and we walked across the back field to a shed by her cottage. As she retrieved a shovel and pick for me, I took in her little garden and home, all well-kept, like the grave yard. Inside, I could see a bright orange blanket covering her tiny bed, and a table with books.

After a few minutes back at the grave, I said, "This is my first time as a grave digger, you know."

"Oh. Well . . . I reckon yah may as well . . . see what it's like. You'll . . . have a hole like this, too . . . one day."

"So I will," I said, and kept digging.

I was surprised when we stopped our work well short of six feet. I said as much.

"That ain't really . . . how it works," she replied. "See, all o' that . . . may be just . . . fine in the big . . . city, but out . . . in these . . . hills, things are. . . different. 'Sides . . . you don't wanna go . . . trying to dig the . . . mountain. These . . . old rocks is . . . hard."

"So they are." I threw the tools over my shoulder, my full-size implements and her cut down versions alike, and we returned to the shed.

The whole process had only taken a couple of hours in spite of rocky ground, thanks mostly to Eleanor's strength. When the tools were stowed, she invited me to follow her for a cold drink. We trekked up a short rise behind her cabin, and over the ridge was a little stream, carrying leaves rapidly toward the branch that ran along one section of Main Street. Turning left, we followed an established trail along to the shoulder where our ridge and the next met, and in the rocky face below us, a spring bubbled forth. Beside it was a large, low-slung promontory that stabbed out of the ridge. Eleanor climbed down with the help of a rope, and I followed. In spite of her ungainly movements, I had the harder time descending. When I finally set foot on the jutting stone, I saw a small cave, only a few feet deep. On the floor was a piece of board upon which sat three up-turned mason jars, without lids. Eleanor proffered one to me even as she took another and held it under a tiny waterfall, just inches down from the source. I followed suit.

"Woo! That's some fine water, clean and cold."

"Oh . . . yes. That bottled . . . stuff ain't the . . . same." She sat on the ledge, letting her bare feet dangle. I fished for my smokes, hung my coat on a nearby branch, and joined her.

"Been in Ravencroft long?" I asked.

"All . . . my life. You?"

"Days to your years."

"Oh. Why?"

"Why what?"

"Why did you come . . . here?"

"Oh," I thought a moment, searching for the best answer for her. "Well, I suppose the price was right."

She frowned again, inciting that horrible transfiguration. "You oughtn't . . . tah lie. I ain't . . . never . . . done you no . . . wrong."

I was taken aback. I stammered briefly before apologizing. "Look," I said, "I'm sorry. I didn't mean to lie. I just don't exactly know how to tell the truth."

"Oh." The grimace faded. "I reckon it must . . . be . . . all citified an' . . . complicated."

"Not really," I admitted with a sigh. "It's basic human nature stuff, I guess. I did some bad things, and, well, my family and I, we aren't really talking right now."

"Oh. But you . . . coulda gone . . . anywhere, justabout." The last came out as one word.

"That's true," I admitted. "I don't know, Miss Eleanor, something about this town just seemed right to me."

"Oh. Well . . . then, I reckon you . . . really been . . . here all along." Eleanor hopped suddenly to her feet. "I . . . gotta go. It was . . . nice tah . . . talk with you."

She scrambled up the rope and was gone. I called "bye" after her, but after a moment of rustling leaves, I was alone in the woods. I drained my water and had another, relishing the purity of it. As I drank, I took in the view: the moss here was bright and dappled with light as the sun slid on toward afternoon. The leaves were bright beside the stream, all golden and orange.

The breeze shifted and picked up, and as I rose to go, it carried the smell of burning wood.

Ravencroft Springs was all right, in places, but I would be unable to savor it while the doubts and shadows remained, and Miss Eleanor Hopewell had only added to their number.

"Cass, I need to ask you a few questions."

Her fingers were splotched with paint as she stood in the living room working on a canvas. It was turning out to be a landscape in alien colors. Reference photographs tacked to the rail of her easel stood out in their natural green tones against the purpley majesty of the painting.

I had driven straight to her house, Dunmore Place, in part because I wanted to see it—and her—by daylight. Returning to Ravencroft had been an easy call; the choice between a life of love and horror, or the horror of a life without love. I didn't believe Ravencroft could possibly be the Arkham of the South, but I knew deep in my marrow that I was on the track of something real.

"Shoot," she said.

I steeled myself, sipped the Irish coffee she had offered, and went directly to the investigation.

"Would you call the people who live here 'evil?' "

Her brush hand, the left, hesitated, but she did not turn. "Some of them maybe, but then I can't say I know what evil is."

"Okay. That's a fair cop. You know the history of the town, the way it has been abandoned or wiped out several times—"

She cut me off. "Several?"

"Yes, several. Something like three times in the eighteen hundreds alone."

"Oh, David, are you getting paranoid? Times were hard back then, and this was a frontier. Indians, illness, all kinds of things could have been responsible for that stuff." Her tone was light, almost dismissive. It provoked my hackles. Her brush clanged as she rapidly tapped it against the inside of the miniature bucket she used for rinsing.

"Fine," I said, maybe a little sharply. "What about the Depression then? Towns all around here were reinvigorated by the Tennessee Valley Authority, why not Ravencroft?"

"Is it that blow to the head? Because you're not making any sense. Maybe I should drive you to the clinic."

"It's a bump. I'm fine and I'm serious. Why did it take so long for Ravencroft to get back on the map after the thirties?"

"I don't know, David, ask FDR. What is it you really want to know?" She wiped the pigment-laden water from her brush and set it aside before sitting beside me. "Are you sure you're all right?"

Our hands intertwined and I was momentarily lost in her eyes.

Ignoring the last question and my pounding pulse, I went on. "What about the stuff in those jars downstairs? What the hell is that stuff?"

"I don't know, David," she said with creased brow. "I hate it down there. It's all just stuff my mom left."

"But they're all over town, Cass! There was even one in my fucking fridge when I moved in. People don't even jar meat anymore!" I was exasperated, my voice was rising. She started to speak, but I cut her off. "And what about that girl, Eleanor Hopewell? She lives in the cemetery, for Pete's sake! She digs graves, Cassandra, and she's just a little girl!"

"She's not quite as young as you think," Cassie answered evenly. "David, look, there are a lot of old families with old traditions in Ravencroft. I don't know who pickles that stuff, or who eats it. I think the jars in Cordelia's place have been there as long as I can remember." Following a deep breath, she took my hands, leaned in closer. "Are you really all right, David?"

I sighed, liberated my right hand to light a smoke. "I think so. I mean, relatively speaking, I'm fine. This place just has me, I don't know, off-balance." I drained the remainder of my spiked coffee and laid back on the couch, eyes focused somewhere beyond the ceiling. Cass still held my left hand.

"Balance is hard to keep sometimes David, and from what you've told me, life's been pretty hard on you lately. Maybe you just need to relax and have some fun. Listen, the Harvest Social is coming up, on Halloween, why don't we go and do some serious line dancing?"

I laughed, and the sound was less hollow than I had expected. "Maybe, though line dancing isn't really my thing."

"I know it's not, that's why it will be good for you. Think about it."

"I will, but first I need you to answer another question." I sat up and looked her in the eye.

"Ye gods!" She tore her hands away and wrung them frantically, screwing up her face into a pinched parody of frustration. "Out with it, then!"

"Why did you tell me the other night that this town is death?"

"I didn't say that, David. I said, 'this town is dead.' Dead, not death. What would that mean anyway?"

"Don't know, that's why I asked. I guess I misheard you." It seemed plausible, but there had been something in her tone that night, and I was sure I had heard it clearly. She was lying. I knew it, but I didn't know how to react.

My face must have betrayed my worry, or tension, or paranoia: her pale brow furrowed and she leaned to kiss my forehead, mumbling, "My poor wounded writer." The smell of her washed over me, and we lost ourselves in each other's desire.

We eventually made our way up to her bedroom in the attic where a wide window looked over the business district. When she fell asleep I stood looking down at the town hall for some time, smoking and doubting myself. I took time to watch Cass dreaming. Her lips curled into a slight smile, then her jaw tightened and the curve of her smile took on menace. When I kissed her eyelids the gentle smile returned.

I left soon after, and made my way downtown, all the while kicking myself mentally for what I was about to do. When I reached the town hall, I looked all around, wishing I still had a mag light instead of the sad little pocket light that now guided me.

The building was somewhere between neo-classical and neo-gothic, composed of Ionic columns and a clock tower. It bore arched windows of leaded glass, and the clock face itself was copper, so in need of polishing that it looked like a looming verdigris eye. The hands had not run their course in years.

Finally satisfied that no one was about, I fished Michael's key out of my pocket and entered the basement. Inside, a short hall accessed doors labeled "Utility," "Clerk," "Stairs," and "Archives." I tried the antique knob of this last door, and found it unlocked.

Inside, plastic crates of unopened mail burdened a long table. My pocket flashlight's beam flicked about the contents, illuminating many different names and postage dates, but all the addresses were in Ravencroft. It finally occurred to me that I myself had gotten no post. UPS and FedEx came, but I had not seen a single U.S. Postal Service vehicle.

Around the table stood rows of bookcases, each with more mail crates on top, but the shelves held a variety of media, including various kinds of ledgers, slide boxes, maps and in the very back of the room, newspapers.

A frantic search commenced, my haste born of the fear of discovery. Three different papers had been archived in the most haphazard fashion, and I scanned headlines and tossed editions into the corner until I found one that interested me and shoved it into the capacious pockets of my trench coat.

Inside of twenty minutes I locked the door of my apartment behind me, retrieved my vodka from the freezer and sat at my kitchen table to peruse my selections.

Michael had spoken rightly: there were indeed two general types of recurrent stories that interested me. The first was a selection of disappearances.

The earliest edition I had found was from 1912 and it reported the story of Isabel Thornton, a schoolgirl who never came home, and briefly of a boy who had vanished a month earlier. From what I gathered, every few months someone simply disappeared. There were reports of locals who had been arrested in the Cove or Knoxville, but I wondered if those were just cover-ups. Sometimes whole families dropped off the radar, never seen again.

I played the back-and-forth in my head: some of them did move, run away, or elope, but not all. Police interviews, pleading parents and milk-carton photos all appeared in those pages.

Somehow the second type of article was weirder. People in Ravencroft saw things in the night. There were reports of ghosts, of banshees, of hellhounds or werewolves. People were accused of witchcraft. An asylum had been built in nineteen eleven because so many residents were going mad. Stories from the fifties implied that some of the people incarcerated there never came out again. One photograph of the place communicated its location to me. What I thought had been a lodge, the big limestone affair farther up Unaka Mountain, had in fact been a madhouse where the insane were committed alongside the terminally ill and the remarkably inconvenient.

Again, I found myself struggling with disbelief. The whole scenario was impossibly dark, like something out of a lost-press horror comic. A cursed mine, a cultist mayor, and beasts on the mountain were too much for even my itinerant sense of disbelief to swallow. Had I really stumbled onto the Arkham of the South? Was I actually still in it? Try as I might, I was unable to dismiss the evidence.

Too stirred up to sleep, I took a drive up to the mine entrance. My gladius lay in my passenger seat and the pistol weighted my coat pocket as I warmed the engine and looked over my map. It looked as though Cass had been taking me to that very spot when the storm had hit us before.

I took my time, driving slowly so that the engine was quiet, and using only my running lights. Leaving the car in the parking lot, I hustled up the path for what must have been a quarter mile before coming to the entrance. A sign declared it closed, to reopen for guided tours in April.

I lit a cigarette, cupping the flame against the gusting wind, and wondered if anyone had ever vanished from a tour, and examined the gate. Formidable black iron, with tightly spaced bars, it loomed behind a chain link fence. Shrouded Masterlocks secured both.

Hearing something move to my right, I spun and aimed my flashlight only to see an opossum slink off into the woods. With a sigh of relief, I turned to go, my flashlight swinging down to light the path.

I squatted down where the gravel gave way to examine what seemed to be several distinct sets of footprints. The path was still muddy from the rain, and there were clear tracks of boots, tennis shoes, women's pumps and even bare feet going both ways—into and out of the mine.

Something glinted in the pocket light's dimming beam: coppery metallic. I scuffed away a layer of wet leaves to find a scattering of discarded mason jar lids beside the path. The discs and rings were wet, but not rusty, and still stank faintly of vinegar.

Walking carefully back down the wooded hillside, I actually drew the pistol from my pocket. Quietly, slowly, I moved as my heart pounded insistently in my chest.

But I reached my car, and then my home, unaccosted. My dreams were troubled by dark myths.

NINE

I spent the following day recovering at home, again. It seemed as though the stress, the doubt, the impossibility of it all tired me more than a good beating ever could. Or maybe it had been the grave digging. I ignored the creeping mold, unopened boxes and dread in favor of a movie marathon featuring the Evil Deads and most of the Friday the 13th run. The absurdity of old school teen horror was somehow lost on me, but it passed the time and shed a stark B-list light on my own situation. More or less.

I didn't really watch them, anyway. My focus wandered often to the windows, beyond which a cold wind blew skittering leaves and dark clouds about the sky. As the afternoon waned, a dark shadow lingered overhead, but it was gone by the time I reached the window. I meandered into the kitchen for a glass and a bottle. An hour later, I went back for the other bottle.

Setting the half-full scotch bottle next to the empty vodka, I sank onto the couch. The sky was fully dark outside as Friday the 13th part Four neared climax and when Sara found her beau, Doug, dead in the shower. As she screamed her way down the stairs, I thought I heard something behind her wailing, and hit mute button. Cawing. Something very near was cawing. There was nothing through the window but wind and a few splashes of heavy rain.

The noise continued. Every few seconds: a long, croaking caw. I threw on my trench, and peeked out the kitchen door. Nothing.

Another caw, and I went upstairs, toward the roof. As I opened the storeroom door, another caw, right on top of me. I ducked instinctively, but nothing flew past. I straightened,

73

creaking, and hit the light switch. There it was, a great grand-daddy of a raven perched on the mannequin's shoulder. Its shining black eyes stood in contrast to the plaster soldier's dusty lenses.

I approached the thing, slowly. As I came, it pecked absently at the ghillie suit of live moss. A windowpane was broken, bits of glass lay scattered around the booted feet. I got quite close before the bird's head cocked as it issued a short, loud croak. I stopped where I stood, about ten feet away, and the bird flapped its wings once, and shifted its weight. It must have been two feet tall, and it occurred to me that I had not noticed another of its kind in my time in Ravencroft.

I stepped back, and the bird pecked an insect from the moss in the mannequin's ear, raising its beak to swallow it down. A millipede, maybe.

It cawed again, three short outbursts, and hopped from the shoulder to the window, and then out. I followed and watched it land in a tree down the street, lit in shining blue by the streetlight. The wind picked up and it took flight again, out of my line of sight.

I went ahead up to the roof anyway, and listened to the pelting rain and blowing wind. As the wind picked up, some taller trees were stripped of their last leaves, sent skirling down the street, piling against curbs and walls.

Halloween morning I woke after ten. A light, persistent cough had settled into my chest, but I smoked with my coffee and toast nonetheless, watching from my wide window as the ghostly shroud of mist faded away to reveal the town. I did a lot of smoking -and more pacing- over the hours that followed.

As evening approached, I stood in the kitchen in black slacks and turtleneck with a gray blazer concealing my pistol, just in case there was trouble, and weighed my options one last time. Snatching up my keys, I made for the door. I didn't want to keep Cass waiting. On the way, I rolled down the windows and enjoyed the last warm afternoon of autumn, ignoring the nagging weight in my chest.

Cassie was waiting on the porch in a blue velvet dress and an awkward smile. I met her on the marble steps with a gentle kiss.

"What's the plan?" I asked.

"I thought we'd take a ride before the social, maybe over to Johnson City."

"What's in Johnson City these days?"

"Well, a good liquor store for one, and a change of scenery for another."

"Sounds good to me, Cass. Let's roll."

Driving the long farm road out of town, then onto I-26 into Johnson City, we listened to the radio dish out generous helpings of southern-fried rock. My attempts to engage conversation were largely unsuccessful. Cassie was intent on the road.

I followed her directions off the interstate and through town to One-Stop Liquor. She had become more forthcoming by the time went in, and we told drinking stories while making our selections: Stoli for me and Hennessy V.S.O.P. for her.

We strolled out of the store, brown bags in hand. When I went to open her door, she pinned me against the car with her body.

"You're a real gentleman, Mr. Writer."

"And you are quite a lady, Miss Cassandra." We kissed again, and I had to tap her thigh with a bottle to remind her I had my hands full. I passed her Hennessy over and opened her door. As I went around to my side, I saw that she was frowning.

"What's wrong?" I asked over the roof. She put a foot into the car, and hesitated briefly before sitting down and closing the door. I followed her into the cabin, but didn't let go of my question. "What is it?"

She put her hand on my thigh. The other fidgeted with her spaghetti strap, and she offered a forced smile.

"I guess I just don't feel like a social tonight."

"We don't have to go," I offered. "We could have some dinner and spend the night in, or see a movie."

"I have to go, David. Al needs help with the food, and everyone will expect me. You can still bow out. I wouldn't blame you."

"Nope."

"Mr. Writer, sir, it's just a bunch of old rednecks and hill people line dancing and drinking 'til all hours. You won't know anyone and I just know you'll hate it." Her gaze flitted away from me and settled on her knees.

"Oh, if it's that bad, count me in. There's no way I'm going to let you suffer that kind of hell with no backup."

With furrowed brow, she nodded. "If you insist, Mr. Writer."

We arrived back in Ravencroft Springs an hour later, and I parked in front of Ophelia's to help with the catering. It was dark by the time we followed Al's old F-150 pickup to the town hall steps. The place was full of life and light, a stark contrast to my previous visits. Many hands helped load the food in, including the Sheriff out of Limestone Cove and mayor Jessica Prater, a tall, ample woman with angular glasses and attitudes.

Chris, Joseph and Jabez, the public works department, were dressed to the nines in black suits and fedoras, red carnations sprouting from their breast pockets.

Al bustled everything to a long table at the far end of the hall, set up in front of the stage where musicians, including old Cordelia were tuning up. The old woman's battered cello was joined by an acoustic guitar, a steel guitar, an upright bass, fiddle, mandolin and some pipes. I could tell watching them mill about that this was your traditional session group: casual but highly skilled and soulful. The gathered musicians had likely been playing together all their lives.

We helped arrange the hot plates and steam pans, and tucked our bottles into Al's private cooler after pouring tall drinks for ourselves. Cass led me by the hand back out the front as the others put out wooden folding chairs and cabaret tables around the perimeter of the hall. In the parking lot, we chatted about the event: how few children ever showed up at these things, how raucous folks would get, and how many drinks were required to survive.

Having drained our glasses, we joined the trickle of hill country socialites on their way in. Well past dark by this time, I snuck a long kiss on the steps before letting Cass pull me inside. The band struck up properly, belting out bluegrass, and soon the hall was full. Cassie had been right: I didn't know any of these people, so I hovered around the catering table and did as I was told.

I recognized more than a few of them, from the diner, mostly, but around town as well. Others hailed from farther out, or up, in the distant reaches of Unicoi County. They seemed like good country folk, Appalachian natives through and through.

After some twenty minutes, Cordelia bowed out for a break. She approached the serving table with an old, brown glass bottle in one hand and a gnarled wooden cane in the other. Setting her bottle on the corner of our table, next to an enormous dish of scalloped corn, she dragged a chair over and bent even further as she settled down into it.

"I'll have me some o' that corn there, if ya don't mind," she said, throat croaking over the music. "And a slab o' ham, too."

I handed her a plate, a napkin, plastic utensils. "Here you go," I smiled.

She nodded and tucked in, sawing voraciously at the ham and shoveling it in between long pulls from her bottle. A low, long belch poured out of her once she had pushed back her paper plate. The odor was something like soured elderberry wine.

"Pardon," she said with a crooked smile. "That's fine eatin' and thank you. Now, you lissen here," she said gesturing me in with a crooked finger. I leaned in, and she leaned forward, straightening up insofar as she was able.

"You be good to our Miss Cassandra, now," she said quietly and clearly. "And you keep clear of my Eleanor, you hear me?" With the last she laid her claw-like hand on my chest, right over my heart. It was cold even through my jacket. As I stared blankly at her, she slowly began to nod. Once, and I watched. Twice, and I nodded with her. A third time, we moved in syncopation, and she pulled her hand away.

She stood, smiled at me with her lips pressed closed, nodded to Cassie, and walked back to the stage, bottle in hand. I watched her go, before smiling weakly at Cass and chucking her plate into the garbage.

The tune that struck up, with Cordelia in the lead, was dark and fast. A young girl, of maybe twelve or thirteen, but with dark makeup at her eyes, took to singing. The lyrics were hard to make out, but only because her voice was so smooth. Though pitched high and more subtly toned, her vocals had a Morrisonesque quality. Behind her, the band pushed a low and throbbing cadence, punctuated by a counterpoint of wailing fiddle and pennywhistle.

Cassie and I poured ourselves drinks freely as the event worked up to its full swing. Within an hour, we were both buzzed, and we were by no means alone. Plenty of beer, moonshine and mountain wine made the rounds, and more than once I caught a whiff of marijuana. The dancing shook the floor, and a fistfight broke out around eight o'clock. Though the Sheriff, an old man, but with broad shoulders and thick arms, put the rabble in their place, the tension had risen.

Not long after the scuffle, Wilton strutted in with Kaleb, who still limped a bit, resplendent in their everyday costume of torn jeans and old t-shirts. I eyed them from my socially elevated position of food provider, and they eyed me right back.

"Dance with me," Cass whispered into my ear, leaning unsteadily against me.

My assent got me yanked straight onto the floor as the band kicked into a spirited reel and I did my best to keep up. Skirts and feet swirled around me, but I soon found the steps and keyed in on the carnivalesque notes of Cordelia Honeycutt's cello.

Jessica Prater stopped the music once to announce the raffle winners; Tom and Adelia McLendon, who received a one hundred dollar gift certificate to Sears. Some minutes thereafter she thanked everyone for coming, many by name.

"This is sure to be the very best Autumn Festival Ravencroft has seen in many years," she said. There was some clapping and shouting, and she went on. "There are many great things about our old-fashioned way, and one of the best is welcoming and honoring those who come to us from the very modern world beyond our little valley. Won't you join me, Mr. Dunbarton?"

I was surprised. Cassie squeezed my hand and pushed me forward, but as I looked back at her, I saw something worrisome in her smile.

"Mr. David Dunbarton has come to Ravencroft Springs to open a new gallery, Constellations, up on Black Ridge Road. Let's welcome this fine young writer and art dealer to our town," she said to the crowd, which erupted in a shout, a quick, sharp 'eeyah' sound, before clapping.

"Thank you," I said over the applause. "It's lovely to be here." Darting away from the mayor and the center of attention, I returned to Cassie.

The music started up again, and the mountain band laid into a set of highland reels.

The flashing smiles and stomping feet were all a distant hum that droned behind Cassandra. Her face became the only clear sight, her breath the only sound.

We danced on and on, song after song. Al appeared once with cups of water, which we drained before stepping back into the line. It eventually became evident that the crowd was thinning and the night wearing on, and still we danced.

Finally, after my feet and legs and lungs were fit to immolate, the music stopped, leaving only a long base thrum in my ears. I staggered, suddenly aware that something was wrong. The music hadn't faded or spiked into crescendo, it had merely stopped. The room was perfectly still around me. I spun unsteadily to take in the faces around me, too close, whispering something so quietly that I heard only that low thrum.

My balance was slipping away, and I swayed in place, turning to seek, unable to find Cassie. Vertigo came moments after, and then a hard crack to the back of my head. I fell, blacking out momentarily.

I awoke for a few seconds, long enough to feel the pistol being torn from its holster under my jacket, long enough to find Cassandra's face, blankly staring down at me. Then, another crack and unconsciousness.

Ten

The voices were distant, muffled, somehow warped. They came slowly into focus as my consciousness returned, the chordal noise distinguishing itself into varied voices.

"We ain't just gonna pickle him?" The voice was male, I think, and young, maybe Kaleb's.

The responder was female. "No, we certainly are not. This David Dunbarton fellow is a strange one."

"He's an asshole!" Wilton, I thought.

"Maybe so," the feminine voice answered him, "but he's got the strangeness in him, and they want him down below. Besides, won't it be nice to watch prissy Miss Cassandra squirm?"

The men laughed. There was a third man, older with a rich, wicked laugh. When he spoke I recognized the voice, and it chilled me. Al said, "Where is she anyway?"

"She is home, tucked neatly into bed with Chris and Jabez looking after her."

"Why ain't we done her yet?" Wilton wanted to know.

"Godammit boy, you know who she came from. We ain't gonna do her, not tonight nor never." I finally recognized the voice of Mayor Prater. She sounded much unlike her earlier self; not just quieter but colder, almost raspy. I imagined Al looking furious. I wanted him ready to tear Wilton to pieces: I wanted him to defend Cass, to be the man she seemed to think he was.

As my vision returned, I blinked rapidly and took in my surroundings. It was dark, and damp, but two of the people who spoke some way down the hall bore flashlights, which flicked occasionally into my cell. Iron bars so cast in shadow

81

across my body were covered in a slimy moss, as was much of the floor. The air was fetid and cloying and I could barely breathe.

That icy voice caught my attention again.

"This is important now, boys, and I'm deadly. If you fuck this up, you will never find The Way."

"What the hell for? How come a damn stranger is worth more than us?"

"How come?" she spat. "I'll tell you how come, you fucking piss-ant. They want him, Unaka wants him, and that's just about all you need to know. If you've got a problem with that and I'll just get you ready for Joe Barron right now. I'm sure he's hankering real good for another slaughter."

Her answer was only silence.

"That's a'right. Now ya'll just have to keep him here for an hour or so. Keep quiet, and keep still, and just keep him here. That ain't hard is it? Good." I heard her walking away, heels clicking sharply on the stone floor. Al's clumping boots followed.

Alone now, excepting myself, they stood in silence down the hall. I heard them shuffling. A lighter flared, and I smelled tobacco smoke. Focusing hard, I could hear nothing, not even a whisper, until a noise from behind startled a gasp from me. Craning my head around as I lay in the dust, I saw a high, barred window in the cell's back wall. There was Smoky Mountain mist drifting in, and a silhouette close to the bars. Squinting against the pale light, I was unable to identify the shadow until it spoke.

"David? Um . . . is that . . . you?"

I didn't want to rise or speak and risk alerting Wilton and Kaleb, but they were too far down the hall to see me. I raised my right hand, waved at Eleanor Hopewell.

Rolling quietly onto my side to face her, I clasped my hands together in silent supplication. The silhouette seemed to shake its head.

"Ah'm . . . real sorry, David. Ah can't . . . help you. Oh," she said, "Ah sure . . . would like . . . to."

With eyes clenched tight, I wanted to shout at her, to ask why.

Her slow whisper came in reply. "Aunt Cordelia . . . she'd have . . . my hide if . . . I got involved in . . . The Way. This is all . . . I can . . . do." Something dropped with a barely audible thump to the dusty floor below the window. "Goodbye . . . David," she said. "Ah'm real . . . sorry."

Again, I pressed my palms together, closed my eyes, all but praying for her help.

When I opened my eyes again, she was gone. "Fuck," I thought.

I rolled back onto my stomach, eased myself onto hands and knees, and painstakingly crawled to see what Eleanor had left me. It had landed too lightly to be a gun, seemed too small to be a knife. As I approached, I could barely make out a leather pouch in the near darkness.

As I reached out for it, a flashlight beam tracked obliquely into the cell. I froze in place, held my breath. I didn't want to draw their attention, at least not until I had Eleanor's gift in hand and a plan in mind. The beam of light slipped away, back down the hall, and there was no indication that they were coming. I scooped up the pouch, and spun painfully on my knees.

Back more or less in place, I raised myself up on my elbows and fingered the leather cords furiously to open my gift. Reaching into the pouch I felt a fine chain and an oddly shaped pendant.

Withdrawing the charm, I peered through the dimness, felt its edges and contours with my fingers. It was a silver sculpt of a bird in flight, a sort of deep relief. The bird hung from its chain facing slightly upwards and to the left. In the dim light, I couldn't make out much detail.

I let it fall back into the pouch in resignation. What Eleanor had given me was only a charm, the kind Ravencroft shops might have sold back in the sixties and seventies for a few measly bucks, the kind of thing an eighth-grader might have given to his sweetheart.

I wondered if it was some kind of talisman, but in spite of all I had seen, I still didn't buy into that sort of thing. What Eleanor intended I could not guess, but there was nothing to be done with her token. I tucked into my hip pocket and sighed quietly to myself.

The toughs approached, the beam of their flashlight skimming over and around me. I closed my eyes and stilled myself.

I expected them to open the cell door and give me hell, but they didn't. To my relief, they stood in the hall and conversed, after eyeing my unmoving shape for a while.

"I hate that bitch," Kaleb said.

"Yah. Me too, man, but what are you gonna do? She's the mayor."

"Yeah, yeah. I hate this fucking place too, though. Hellhole is what this is. You know they say a bunch of people got killed here."

"Oh, fuck me, Kaleb. Who gives a shit? Ain't you figured it out? Can't you come to grips? We're from Ravencroft. Ain't gonna be long before we're the ones doin' the killing, and you still talk like some fool from the Cove who don't know no better."

"Wait, you mean you're really going down there? You really believe in The Way?"

I was listening hard now. Kaleb's voice had descended into a whisper.

"Course I do, and so do you, dipshit. It's real, and you know it. You've fuckin' well seen it."

"Yeah, but why? I mean why us, why here? I don't want no part of this thing."

"But you are part of it," Wilton answered, his tone turning conciliatory. "There's nothing you can do, dude. If you leave, you'll come back. How many have you seen do it? Everybody, right? Every sonuvabitch who ever left here came back. This mountain's in their blood, it's in your blood.

"Ain't no choice but to embrace it. One day, we will change. Hell, we might even get real lucky and change into something goddamn awesome. When we finally take the Way Below," this was said with solemn reverence, "you'll see. We will live forever, Kaleb, and it ain't gonna be no bullshit afterlife either, we will literally live forever. And one day the darkness will come and The Way Below will just be The Way. When that happens, we're gonna be on top! We'll be the high priests of Unaka and rule the fuckin' world."

"You really believe every word of that, don't you?" I asked. I had risen on unsteady legs during Wilton's speech and stood in the middle of my cell. "Is that why you beat the shit out of me? Because you didn't want me in your stupid redneck cult?"

I thought I might get a rise out of them, and Kaleb did look ready to jump, but his big friend steadied him with a hand on the shoulder.

"It doesn't matter now, David," he said. "You're going down into the mountain, and that's that."

"Why? What's down there?"

Kaleb laughed and said, "Oh, don't worry, it ain't like hell or nothin'."

Wilton leapt at another chance at oratory. "I'll tell you what's down there, David. The Way Below is down there, the long-lost secret to eternal motherfucking life. But see, that ain't for everyone, now. You've got to have the blood of Unaka in you, got to be one of his own to go on. You, well, we know they ain't gonna eat you, so there's only one thing I can recon they'd need you for. Ain't many that can hold out down there for very long who ain't already on The Way, and every once in a while, we needs us some kiddies round here."

I cut him off, "You're talking shit. They're going to use me for what? Sex?"

"It ain't what you think. It ain't nice. You can't imagine it, what Those Who Have Gone are like, so don't even try. Don't matter none. It's time."

Kaleb produced a large key, from which dangled a rabbit's foot. I approached as he went to unlock the old cell door.

"Don't you try anything," he said, "I'm just about sick of you, and I might have to get rough."

I smiled, and when he had unlocked the door, I kicked it hard. He sprawled backwards as the rusty, slimy hinges swung the door wide. His flashlight rolled off against the far wall, illuminating only a swath of moldy plaster. I rushed to get through, but Wilton stepped into the opening. I elbowed him in the chest with all my strength. Even though the air left him, he managed to swing a leather sack over my head. Inside was a sickly sweet smell, less noxious than the air of my cell but perhaps more dangerous: chloroform.

"So cliche," I thought, "but it's better than another beating."

Holding my breath, I struck out madly with fist, elbow and knee, but Wilton shoved one forearm in my throat, his other hand holding the bag to the back of my head. His breathing was deep and fast as he tried to get back the air my elbow had cost him.

We struggled in the cell's doorway, the big youth bearing down on me, forcing me into the bars and tearing my lower back open against a hinge. Knowing my time was short, I fired several quick punches toward his groin. It seemed as though the tide might turn when Kaleb hit me in the kidney with what must have been his flashlight—my flashlight. I took a deep inadvertent breath, and consciousness began to wane. I pushed with all my might, but my muscles burned and my lungs starved. Too weakened to resist, Wilton spun me around and slammed me into the wall, driving out what little air I had retained. After a moment of vertigo, I was unconscious again.

Eleven

The sound of screaming woke me some time later. It was Cass. Her voice was hoarse, cracked, splitting at the edges from too much wear.

"You can't take him. Let him stay up here with me!"

The answering voice was quiet, indistinct. My returning senses told me that I was face-down in gravel with the hood still over my head and my hands roped behind my aching back.

"Damn you, Jess. You can't let me have anything, can you?"

This time I could make out the reply. "You have The Way Below, Cassandra. That is all any of us need. I'm sick to death of your constant petulance." I could tell she was coming nearer. Two pairs of hands hauled me more or less upright by the elbows.

The bag was yanked away and there was Jessica Prater, so close I could smell her over the fading sweetness of the chloroform: a subtle stench of decay hovered under high-end perfume. Her lips were wet. A low dissonant throb sounded in the chilled night. Our feet, everyone's feet, were swallowed in a clammy mist.

"The Way Below tells us all we need to know, child. You're born to it and you can't turn away, no matter your intent. Just think of your mother."

"Leave my mother out of this! Leave me out of it. I want out!"

"You only believe that because this man has caught your little heart. If we take him Below, then why wouldn't that tender heart follow?"

Cassandra's reply was quiet. Her voice tremored. "Because you'll kill him."

Jessica stepped into me as the men held me steady. To avoid her closeness I swiveled my head to the right, seeing Al, his face set in a vacant grimace. I turned to see who held my right arm, but Jessica caught my chin, and held it with surprising strength. Her breasts were hard against me, but there was no heat in them. Something moved against my chest where we were pressed together, pushing at me. I glared back into her eyes defiantly.

"You're fucking kidding me," I said slowly. "You drugged me and now you're going to take me into the abandoned mine to rape and kill me? What are you, a goddamn Rob Zombie character?"

"Open the gates," was her reply, given as she turned away, allowing me to finally see past her.

Cassandra's dress was torn, her right ankle bloody. She stood off to the left, near the gate, and Wilton and Kaleb stood beside her, ready to grab her if ordered. All around us stood the people of Ravencroft Springs and my senses reeled as I took them in.

Townsfolk, most of whom I knew only from the diner, stood all around in a loose formation encircling the parking lot. Flashlights, oil lanterns and even a couple of torches lit the scene, the medley of light partially blinding me, but I could just see that most were naked.

Cordelia sat on the gray stone above the mine entrance with her cello. She leaned against a gnarled tree, from which hung a rusty lantern. In that flickering light, I made out her pale and naked body, deflated as though she had no ribs. The old man from my first visit to the diner stood not far behind Cass, his wide belly scaled like a snake's, his missing ears clearly no accident.

Chris Calloway had finally removed his shades, and watched me with tiny, milky-white eyes as the first gate opened behind him. My pistol was tucked into his belt. The man on my left arm was Joseph, the older brother, smiling from under his fedora. A serpentine tongue dashed out and scented my ear, and Joseph laughed.

In the background, Jabez leered from the van's passenger window, waving his carnation and laughing.

Joseph grunted to Al, and they stepped me slowly forward as the wrought iron inner gate swung open. The clang echoed in the damp air.

My heart pounded and my ears began to ring.

"Now or never," I whispered to myself. I slumped and squatted low as though collapsing, and then pushed up hard with my legs as my captors shifted to support my weight. I hurled my elbows up and out as I rose, and found the bindings allowed enough motion to do some damage. Joseph's hat flew off, revealing hairy bat-like ears as he staggered back with a broken nose. Al fell where he stood, gasping for air, his gimp leg writhing under threadbare jeans.

I heard Cassie screaming and looked to see her struggling against the toughs, who prevented her from coming to my aid. She managed to put a knee to Wilton's groin as I charged Jessica Prater, trying to tear my arms free.

She turned to run as I tore through the dry-rotted rope and reached for her, hoping to put her between me and my gun, now surely readied to shoot me in the back.

When the shot went off, I thought I was done for, even though I didn't feel it. I had heard it happens that way sometimes, but I knew at once that it wasn't me that had been hit. Cassie was there with me suddenly, so relieving me by her presence that we all but tripped over the fallen mayor. Jessica writhed at our feet, gasping and choking.

Michael Brennan emerged from the darkness, rifle readied. The locals parted as he walked steadily into the ring of light.

"Drop the gun, Calloway," he demanded.

"Fuck you, old man. We don't need no gatekeepers here anymore."

Another shot rang out, this one from afar, and Chris jumped as the gravel at his feet exploded.

"Cara's up on the widow's walk, ya see. She's a good

shot, ain't she, son? So, let's just drop the goddamn gun, why don't we?"

Chris chucked the pistol a few feet away from him and I scooped it up, leveling the iron sight on his forehead.

Cordelia Honeycutt played that same low thrum from above the gates, and I swung the gun up at her.

"Easy, David." Cassandra had tears in her eyes, and again I was suddenly drawn into her. Michael speaking behind me and the eerie notes of the cello sounded as though they were underwater, and Cassandra smiled through her tears.

"It's all right, Mr. Writer." Her eyes were hollow, though wet.

I could only stammer in reply.

Michael shook me from behind, bringing the world beyond Cass into focus. There were noises coming from inside the mine now, and Cordelia's music had become a husky scream of impossible cadence.

"Let's go, boy. Leave her."

I stood my ground, but turned to him. "No way. The mayor's dead, we've got the guns, let's take her with us."

"No, David. I have to stay," she whispered.

"What? No fucking way. Come on." I pulled at her hand, but she didn't shift an inch, as though rooted to the mountain.

"I can't. I never could. You know that."

"This is insane. It's impossible, and you don't have to be part of it," I insisted.

"No, David," Cass and Michael said in unison.

"Look around, son," said Michael.

I did. The townies and hillfolk were gathered in a tightening circle around us, Al, Wilton, and Kaleb among them. They dripped with moisture, and their eyes were hollow. The Public Works Department was dragging Jessica's body to their van. Chris had slipped away to join his fellows while I spoke with Michael.

"We'll just blast our way out," I said. "Please, Cass. Please come with us."

"I just can't, David. Jessie was right, I am born to The

Way Below." She shook her head, looking at her shaking hands with paint still on them. "But it can still be all right, David. Michael saved us."

"Not if those twisted fuckers get their hands on us!" Al was just a couple of feet away. The denizens had begun to mutter a low susurrus, punctuated with the same "eeyah" they had issued back at the town hall. "We've got to move."

"Silence!" Cassandra called out sharply. The music ceased and the crowd around us stopped, swaying vacantly in the silence.

"Go to your homes now, and leave Those Who Have Gone to me. I will take David below myself."

"What the fu–" I started. It was Cordelia's hoarse roar that cut me off.

"We do not listen to you, girl! You are but a Gatekeeper with only one foot on The Way."

Michael and I shared a glance, communicating our mutual ignorance. His rifle pointed at Cordelia from the hip.

Cass yelled up at her. "You know who my father was! You know that I'm mayor, now that my aunt Jessica is dead."

"Who the fuck cares?" I was shouting at her.

"I do!" she shouted back, and the mist swirling at our feet rippled with her vehemence. "I can never leave here now, not even to visit my family, not for any damn reason. I am the leader of this community, now. The Way Below never meant anything to me before, David, not really, but now it does. You killed Jessie, you idiot," she spat at Michael, "and now I'm the only one left."

"The only what?" I demanded.

"The only one above who shares Unaka's blood, the last descendant of the Cherokee shamans who worshipped the dark spirit of this mountain. I'm heir to the throne, voice of Unaka, The Dweller Below. My word is law."

With this last she stared defiantly up at Cordelia, who offered no rebuttal.

"I'm bound to the mountain ghost, and to the ancient customs. But you can stay with me, David. I know it sounds crazy, I do, but it's going to be all right. You only have to go below for a year, and they cannot defy me. They can't hurt you."

"Don't believe that, son," Michael urged in a whisper.

"Why would I want to go in there, Cass? What the hell are you thinking?"

Her expression betrayed hurt and frustration. "We can be together this way, David. You can come back in a while, and we can marry if you want. I'll be mayor and you can be whatever you want. You just won't be able to leave here." The strain in her heart had shredded her voice, so that her pleading sounded more like shrieking.

I stood stunned, trying to make sense of it all as November's first storm heralded a thunderclap in the distance, and the wind picked up, swirling about our heads.

"Why not?"

"Because your soul, your will, is bound to Unaka. He will summon you back if you stay away too long, compel you." I tried not to think about the fact that he already had.

Cordelia spoke, "He whispers to me even now. He hungers."

"Shut up," Cassie spat. "David, look, I never imagined it could really be possible. It just didn't occur to me, but Michael and Cara did us a favor, in spite of themselves. Stay with me. I can even take you down myself, but to let you change your mind once through that gate is impossible. I, too, can hear Him."

"Don't do it, David!" Michael could see me thinking, still caught up in my disbelief and dilemma. He raised his voice against the surging wind, which now cast skirls of leaves flying between us. "It will change you, son, make you like them. You will rot away from the inside and turn into a monster. You can't believe that's best."

"I do," I said finally. "I choose her." I threw my gun to the ground and took her hands in mine.

The wind rose again, a dull roar amid the branches. I looked down to see that it did not shift the mist. The trees, though, swayed fiercely, and a lantern hung on one nearby branch swung free and crashed to the gravel, spilling flaming oil along the ground.

Cass smiled at me—a genuinely happy, not at all awkward smile, warm in the firelight—and turned with me to the gate. As we passed the chain link, I turned to wave back at Michael. He looked away, rifle hanging slack in his hand. The townsfolk clustered around him, watching us. A few steps later, I could hear them in the tunnel: The Ones Who Had Gone. Stale air carried scratching, whispering, and a chorus of indescribable noises out of the depths. Cordelia thrummed her cello overhead, smiling as I looked up.

We were just two steps from the iron gate when the distant crack of gunfire reached my ears.

Michael cried out behind me before I realized what happened. For an interminable moment, I watched her fall, the blood gushing from a bullet wound. The spray arced forward as she went down, and the mist swallowed her up. Cara had shot my love through the heart. When time realigned itself and I caught up to gravity, I fell to my knees beside her and rolled her over, futilely trying to staunch the flow of her life's blood. There was too much. The exit wound over her heart pulsed only once more under my palm as I tried to hold death at bay. She was gone, and suddenly, I knew that the truth of Unaka and The Way was irrelevant. Whether ancient cult or shared hallucination, The Way had taken my last hope, left her essence a thick, red-black sheen on my hands.

Cordelia struck up her lunatic reel suddenly, cackling over the thrumming cello. Outside the tunnel, the people of Ravencroft descended on Michael.

"I'm sorry, David," he screamed as Wilton drove him to the ground.

I scrambled to my feet, rushing to help as Kaleb and others kicked the fallen man, but something caught my ankle. It squeezed hard, and the pain and cold of its stony grip paralyzed me. I was suddenly and painfully on the ground, clutching at the moist, gravelly dirt, coughing as cloying mist fouled my lungs.

Things moved past me, out of the tunnel. I could see something of them as they entered the ring of light outside, some pale and bloated, others bone-thin, still others oozing slime from mouths, ears, and eyes. One thing only they had in common: not one of them really resembled a human being. A chorus of screams erupted as the creatures met with the hillfolk and villagers of Ravencroft Springs.

Cara Brennan fired a few more shots as the thing dragged me down the tunnel. High caliber bullets sparked off the tunnel walls. The last ricocheted across my thigh, and the searing agony restored my will. I struggled to right myself and twisted round to see a translucent hand, sooty and wide-fingered locked to my ankle. I managed to lean forward into a sitting position and strike that clammy grasp. With a fierce kick, I was free, and scrambled back outside. The fire had spread, catching on the leaves, and cast a strange glow through the mist.

Michael and Kaleb were back to back, fighting off a group of small, impossibly twisted things with gaping maws. The boy had somehow gotten his hands on my pistol, and they fired wildly at the swarming creatures.

Chris lay near the entrance, neck twisted brutally, a gray-green apelike creature tearing at his entrails.

Al stood with Wilton and three other men from town, backs against the van as creatures surrounded them, pale and impossibly mutated. Armed only with knives and tools, they fought valiantly, but Those Who Have Gone were powerful, infinitely varied, and apparently ravenous. A bloated female thing with a shark-like maw in her belly wrestled one of the townsfolk down. When Wilton crushed her skull with his crowbar, she kept clawing at the fallen man, drawing limb after limb into her slavering torso.

Jabez chucked a glass jar out of the van's passenger window. It shattered audibly in spite of the din of gunshots and screams. Several of Those Who Have Gone turned toward the sound, sniffing hungrily. More jars followed, scattered all about, and those monsters not already engaged dove toward them, scrabbling in the gravel, hands and faces buried in the mist as they consumed the spilled meats.

As I stumbled forward, the thing in the mine grabbed at me again, clutching about my waist with thick arms. I grabbed onto the wrought iron inner gate with my left hand and beat uselessly at the arms with my right. Its strength was too much, and it pulled me away from the gate. I drove my elbows back into it, striking at rubbery flesh, twisting furiously in its grasp. I writhed around, beating and shoving against my captor, until I could see what I was fighting: a genuine old-fashioned horror show. The thing stood some four feet high, but a wide, thick, slug-like body trailed out behind it. Its flesh was rubbery, slick with mucus. Atop its vaguely human torso was a head, featureless save for a trio of long tentacle eyestalks. I grabbed two of them, squeezing tight to keep my hold, and pulled with all my strength in opposing directions. There was a tearing sensation, and the central stalk danced wildly, striking at my face and chest. The arms released my waist to grab at my arms, but I was already accelerating out of the mine. I got clear of the chain link fence, in spite of my screaming thigh.

I limped toward Michael, who now stood alone against the two remaining little creeps. Kaleb lay writhing on the ground, clutching at a deep gash across his face. I grabbed one of the things up by its too long neck, lifted it high in the air, and brought it down face-first in the gravel. Releasing my grip, I stomped on its head before it could rise.

Cordelia shrieked on the ridge above, and I looked up just as she hurled her lantern at me. I dove aside and the missile crashed to the ground at the last creep's feet, engulfing it in flames. Michael's leg caught, too, and he dropped heavily to the ground, rolling and patting. It was extinguished by the time I reached him, and I helped him to his feet.

"Thanks, son," he offered as Cordelia hit a long, shrieking chord on the cello. I could no longer see her in the darkness above.

"Thank me later," I said. "Let's get the fuck out of here."

"My truck's just down the road," he said, and we went as fast as his old legs and my shot one would carry us.

The van started up then, and we somehow found it in ourselves to go a little faster, and had just turned the truck around in the road when headlights appeared behind us. As the tires spun gravel out in a spray, I turned to see Al bearing down on us at the van's wheel, Jabez laughing in the seat behind him.

It slammed into us, rocking the old Chevy and wrenching my neck. I turned around and set my hands against the dash. Michael stood on the accelerator, and we pulled away, snaking down the rutted gravel track.

The van stayed right with us, threatening to tap us again at every turn, but we soon hit pavement, and began to pull ahead of our pursuers. A few turns and we slid across wet leaves onto the main drag.

"We've got to get to Cara," Michael shouted in his adrenaline-fueled desperation.

"Great," I replied a little more calmly. "You've got more guns at home, right?"

"You bet your ass!" He turned to smile at me.

"No! Look out!" I screamed as a figure appeared in the headlights. His attention snapped back to the road. A girl in a ragged flowery dress stood in the middle of Main Street.

"Eleanor! What the—" I was cut off as Michael yanked at the wheel.

The tires slipped against the wet leaves lining the roadway, and the Chevy slid out of control. I reached out my left hand to Michael's shoulder, holding him back protectively as I saw it coming: Ophelia's Diner. The truck leapt the crumbling curb and plunged through the diner's windowed brick front. Glass shattered and mortar flew. We penetrated the dining area, scattering tables and chairs, and finally slammed to a standstill against the counter. Steam erupted from the buckled hood, and the engine stalled.

Michael sat slumped against the wheel, blood seeping from his face. I levered him up and back: his nose was broken, and his right eye was blooming black and purple, but he was breathing.

Extricating myself from the truck, I scrambled over the wreckage of masonry, tables and two-by-fours to the sidewalk. Eleanor was gone, and the van had slid to a halt only ten yards away. Al stood waiting as Joe and Jabez debarked from the side doors.

I ran to the driver's door, tore it open, and shook my friend for all I was worth.

"Michael! Come on, they're right there!" Nothing. I shook harder. "Let's go already, old man!" I screamed in his face, and his eyes fluttered open. He shook his head, reached under the seat, and handed me an old revolver.

I fired a couple of shots in the van's general direction, and the denizens dove and ran for cover. The time it gained was enough to help Michael from the truck and get us limping through the wrecked diner toward the back door.

We pushed through, and hustled down the alley. I looked back once to see Jabez following us out. He pointed as he issued an ear-piercing shriek, his mouth open impossibly wide and revealing rows of jagged teeth. I fired two more shots and he ducked back behind the door.

"It's only a block now," I reassured Michael, who panted along beside me. He nodded and turned the corner. I followed him around, and Providence House loomed up the hill, a few windows and the widow's walk glowing with an eerie blue light.

I stopped, and Michael turned around. He tugged at my sleeve, saying, "It's just blue lights– they don't glare as much." I started forward again, heavy with misgivings in spite of his explanation.

We were halfway across the postage stamp lawn when a rapport rang out above us. Behind, a cry as Jabez fell in the slick street, blood pouring from his belly.

We went on, and I hazarded a last glance before closing the door behind me. Joe was dragging his little brother to cover as the van edged slowly around the corner, Al hunched low over the wheel. Another shot rang out and chips of stone flew from a retaining wall as Jabez's legs vanished behind it.

I slammed the door and threw the bolt. When I turned, Michael slouched against a display case, his skin gray.

"Are you all right?" I rushed to him. As I placed a hand on his shoulder, he heaved himself upward, took a shallow breath, and nodded toward the hall. I helped him along to the back room, where Arthur paced between the kitchen doorway and the dutch door through which we entered. He fell into heel beside Michael as the man opened a cabinet in the wall beside the fireplace. He tossed me a shotgun and grabbed one for himself.

I racked a shell and tried to smile at the old man, watching him lean against the cabinet, filling the pockets of his coat with ammunition before handing me the box.

Dumping the remainder into my trench coat, I nodded toward one of the big wingback chairs. "Why don't you have a seat," I offered, "and I'll go check on Cara."

"No!" he almost shouted. "I'll go too. We stay together."

So we did, and I followed him up creaking, narrow stairs, first to the upstairs hall, and then on up to the jumbled attic, where a hatch communicated with the rooftop. The narrow widow's walk that surrounded the roof was an oddity in this part of the world, but I was glad of it as Michael stepped out. I thought it would provide an excellent position to defend ourselves long enough to plan our next move.

But as I stepped out, one hand on the railing to support my injured leg, lightning flashed to the east, over Unaka's shoulder, and revealed a great dark shape tearing out of the sky. Michael had seen it too, and we both shouted to Cara, who ducked as we both fired our twelve gauges over her head. With the light gone, we wondered if we had hit it, driven it off maybe. But Cara was suddenly snatched off the roof, screaming. The great thing carried her, its buffeting wings adding to the storm, directly over our heads. Michael reached out to her as she passed, her eyes pleading. A tear fell on my cheek, and she was beyond us. I turned and watched, firing one more shell before the darkness swallowed her.

A sudden crash of wood and glass alerted me that the house had been entered, and I turned to make for the hatch. Michael leaned against the steeply pitched dormer, clutching at his chest, his face frozen in abject sorrow.

"Come on," I shouted. "We might be able to find her."

"No." I could barely hear him over the wind, but he shook his head and stood upright, straighter and taller than I had ever seen him. He held out his shotgun to me, and when I took it, he pitched himself over the low railing onto the lawn below.

"Fuck! Michael!" I screamed down at his broken body, dropping the second gun.

Al pulled the van forward, slammed it into park, and stepped out into the wind, and I fired at him, peppering the side of the van with shot. He slid back behind the door, but didn't go back in, so I leveled the shotgun more carefully and fired again. This time, the shot connected, and Al's left shoulder reddened as he slumped to the ground.

I turned to climb back through the hatch when Joe Pelphry hit me in the gut with the butt of the dropped shotgun. I fell to my knees, losing hold of my weapon and gasping for air. He leveled his barrel inches from my eyes.

"Get up, boy," he said. His voice was high-pitched, nasally. "Get the fuck up now!" The last word, a ragged shout, rang in my ears. I got up.

"That's real good now, son. Listen, you done gave us a heap of trouble tonight. I sure do wish you'd make this real easy for me and fight back. Why, I could pitch you right off this here roof, and nobody'd know no better. You could have a nice rest down there with your friend."

His tongue flicked out, darted about his lips, and slicked back in.

"No? Well, that's gonna be okay too, cause we got a right treat in store for you, ol' son, a right treat!"

He stepped half out of the hatch, motioned me in with the shotgun.

I glared back defiantly, but I was tired, so goddamn tired. I went, and he led me downstairs, and then outside, shotgun in my back all the while. Al was waiting by the van, and as we approached, he limped to the back. He opened the doors and Joe jabbed me with the shotgun. I climbed into the open cargo space. The doors closed behind me, and they climbed in the front. One of them clicked on the dome light, and I saw Jessica Prater laid out on the metal floor, her skin going rapidly gray and her face twisted into a mockery of outrage. Her left eye was missing, presumably an exit wound.

Al started the van up and drove, while Joe climbed into the back, kneeling over Jessica's head. He laid the shotgun across his chest and drew a prodigious bowie knife from his boot.

"Yessir," he keened. "Yes, indeed, this is something real special right here. We figure, Al an' me, that for all this trouble you done caused, and all them people you done hurt, well, you're goin' down all right, but we're gonna see you do some sufferin' for ourselves first."

"Do your worst, you inbred fuck!" I spat.

"That's real good, son. They're gonna just love you down below."

He took his knife, slid the blade smoothly into Jessica's blouse near her waist and drew it back up, severing the threads of her buttons. He tucked the blade back into his boot, and tugged her shirt open, exposing large, lumpy, unbound breasts with nipples dark as the night sky.

"That's something else, ain't it? Look at those! Hoo-boy! Come on, have a closer look."

I stared back blankly. I had felt those tits pressed against me once, and preferred to avoid an encore. He leveled the shotgun, and I crawled slowly forward, slipping once on the metal panel floor as the van took a turn onto a gravel road.

Joe laughed. "Come on now, boy, she ain't getting' no warmer!"

Al chuckled from the driver seat.

I steeled myself in spite of my exhaustion. I would fight to the last. I had lost a lot that night: my love, my friends, even my hope. There was still a chance I could get out of it, though, and oh what a book I'd write then.

But as soon as I came level with the corpse's statuesque bust, Joe brought his barrel down on the top of my head. Fighting the onset of unconsciousness, I slumped forward momentarily over her chest, and something shot from her breast, a writhing black thing, thick-bodied but bearing a host of wispy tentacles. These grabbed at my coat and shirt to draw the thing close to my chest, but I threw myself backwards and grabbed at it with both hands.

Joe laughed, a high, horrible sound. "Hoo-boy!" he exclaimed. "This sure is a night to remember!"

"Damn right," I told him, struggling to my feet and heaving the wiggling black thing at him with all my strength. I tore several tentacles free from their mooring, and they fell limp against my chest as the slug-like parasite slapped into Joe's chest with a wet thud.

He scrambled to draw his knife as the hundreds of tentacles wrapped around him. He cut frantically at them, splitting himself open even as he severed them, but it was too late. Drawn tight against his chest, the thing burrowed right into him, vanishing into a basketball sized hole in his ribcage. He fell and writhed, issuing a handful of ear-shattering screams as the van bounced up the winding graveled track.

I met Al's glance as he looked back, followed his eyes to the shotgun. I rose from my position near the back doors, went to dive for it, but he slammed on the breaks and the van went skidding sideways, threatening to roll before crashing into something with a screech of metal.

Thrown about like a rag doll, I shook my head to clear my vision, and when I dove again for the shotgun, I grabbed it just in time to see Al slamming the driver door behind him.

I checked the gun and took a deep breath, ready to follow him out the same door, when I heard something scrape like a claw along the side door right beside me. Turning, I saw a mass of distorted flesh pressed against the window, clawing and murmuring hungrily.

A window cracked, and a dry, segmented tentacle shot

in toward me. I fired the shotgun, severing it and letting the recoil throw my hunched body toward the front of the van. I shuttled the shell and fired again as another tentacle and warty, three-fingered hand wrenched the side doors free.

Glancing through the windshield, I saw that the van had come to rest sideways against the mine's inner gate. The hood was wrenched open. I fired one more shell and threw the gun at the beasts now pressing into the cargo space.

I stepped over Jessica's body, making for the driver's door when her other parasite leapt. I looked down a fraction of a second too late, just in time to see the worm thing erupt from her black nipple, its fine tentacles snaking into my pants, pulling it toward my crotch.

I screamed, hurling my fists against it. When the hairs found their way past my clothes, they penetrated into my belly, shooting through me with a searing agony. I struggled to hold the slug at bay, but a squat creature, seemingly all folds and flaps of greasy flesh slapped me.

I looked up for a brief moment, horrified at the mass of mutated bodies pressing into the van, hungry for my soul as well as my flesh.

My strength and desperation abandoned me. I was too weak to fight on, and in a flash the grubby parasite was inside me, filling me with ichor and shadows. I fell limp, breathing shallowly, eyes fluttering as the cold darkness of The Way Below spread through me.

Those Who Have Gone gathered me up, gently. My parasite's pain gave way to soul-draining numbness as they passed me along, hand to claw down into the mine.

The indelible darkness of The Way Below swallowed me up. As I went down, I remembered, like the fragment of a dream, the token Eleanor had offered me. My weakened, jostling hand reached into my pocket, drew forth the bag. I hugged it close to my chest as I fumbled to open it, to draw out the little talisman.

Whatever else awaited me in Unaka's depths, there was already one of those things inside me, I reasoned drunkenly as the pervasive numbness spread. I snapped the chain free and let it fall. The silver bird, I swallowed, using the very last of my strength to choke it down. Arms falling limp to my sides, head lolling, I descended into the mine.

In the ancient caverns beneath Unaka Mountain, where a society of blasphemous shadow mocks the world above, I would go on. I would continue not as myself, and not quite as a mindless beast. I would persist, struggling to see the light of day once more, until finally that hope, too, would die, tortured by the impossible weight of eons.

About the Author

Born in southern Missouri, and traveling the American southwest throughout his early life, Logan L. Masterson became rooted in ideas rather than places. Fantasies and imageries are his stock-in-trade. His tools are intuition, observation, vocabulary and rhythm. Well, those and a good word processor. Look for his stories "Clockwork Demons" in Capes & Clockwork, and "Shadow of the Wolf" in Luna's Children II, both from Dark Oak Press. A published poet and arts journalist, he lives in Nashville, Tennessee with five dogs, two turtles, and a lovely wife.

THE ALL-NEW *WILD* ADVENTURES OF

DOC SAVAGE

Doc Savage:
The Desert Demons

Doc Savage:
Horror in Gold

Doc Savage:
The Infernal Buddha

Doc Savage:
The Forgotten Realm

Doc Savage:
Death's Dark Domain

Doc Savage:
Skull Island

30246431R00065

Made in the USA
San Bernardino, CA
09 February 2016